Cara Lockwood ████████████ █████████
author of more th██ ██████teen books, in█████ding
I Do (But I Don't), which ██ ██ made into a Lifetime
Original movie. She's wr█████████████████████
for young adults, and has ███████████████████
into several languages ar █████████████████
raised in Dallas, Cara nov ███████████████████
husband and their five ch████. ██████████████
her at caralockwood.com, "friend" her on Facebook,
facebook.com/authorcaralockwood, or follow her on
Twitter, @caralockwood.

If you liked *Look at Me* why not try

Unleashed by Caitlin Crews
Play Thing by Nicola Marsh
King's Price by Jackie Ashenden

Also by Cara Lockwood

No Strings

Discover more at millsandboon.co.uk.

LOOK AT ME

CARA LOCKWOOD

MILLS & BOON

First Published in Great Britain 2018
by Mills & Boon, an imprint of HarperCollins*Publishers*
1 London Bridge Street, London, SE1 9GF

© 2018 Cara Lockwood

ISBN: 978-0-263-93239-3

MIX
Paper from
responsible sources
FSC C007454

This book is produced from independently certified FSC™ paper
to ensure responsible forest management.
For more information visit www.harpercollins.co.uk/green.

Printed and bound in Spain
by CPI, Barcelona

For the love of my life, my husband, PJ.

CHAPTER ONE

CHLOE PARK STARED at her laptop as she sat at her kitchen table in her roomy north Chicago condo. She fanned her face, desperately trying to get a breeze from her open window. Outside, the June heat pushed the temperature up beyond eighty-five degrees and the noon sun beat mercilessly down on her brick building. Soon, she'd have to break down and call someone to repair her AC, but not yet. Not with her bank account hovering near zero until the end of the week when she expected the arrival of her next freelance check. Chloe tried once more to focus on a work email, but the high-pitched squeal of a truck's old brakes drifting in through her open window broke her concentration. She tried to ignore it, focusing on her screen and the last few sentences she'd need to write before she could hit Send. Then came the sound of metal clanging against metal.

"Really?" she asked her apartment, feeling as though everyone were conspiring against her to get no work done. She had at least five client social media accounts to update and a proposal to send out

to a new corporate client who needed freelance social
media updates *now*. But she couldn't focus on any of
that. Chloe abandoned the email, frustrated, as she
swiped a bit of sweat from her brow. This heat! Ugh.
She hated it. And the noise outside didn't help, but
she also knew if she closed that window her condo
would turn into a brick oven. The clanging was replaced by the voices of men, made louder by the echo
effect of the small alley.

She lived in a small building of just five units,
each stacked on top of the other in an old factory
renovated for condos but originally built in the 1920s.
She lived at the top of their building, on floor four,
in between an office building to the south and to
the north a condo building that was being gutted
and repurposed.

Unable to resist any longer, she grabbed the can of
Coke from her table and went to her window, glancing out to see a small white moving truck in the alley
beneath it, and one mover who struggled to slide a
heavy metal ramp out from the open back.

New neighbor? she wondered, and immediately
knew which one. Had to be the building across the
street, the one she'd seen construction crews head
in and out of as they gutted it and redesigned the
three-flat. The building was made of solid brick with
a faint Herron and Co. logo on the side. No windows faced her, except three on the top floor and a
single lone window on the second. Those had been
the old offices of the executives running the com-

pany. She heard it had once been a cold storage facility back in the early 1900s. This explained the garage doors below narrow enough to fit the horse-drawn carriages that came to pick up deliveries, and the first floor, which was entirely bricked in. Someone told her a condo owner decided to renovate the fourth floor back in the 1980s, adding in windows that looked out on the alley between them. Still, the old icehouse was one of many reasons she loved Chicago, where new lived beside old, modern beside antique and old buildings like this one found new life.

The neighboring building was big enough for three condos, but as far as she knew, the entire building had been empty since she'd moved in eight months ago. There'd been construction crews coming and going, and the rumor from her downstairs neighbor—a Realtor—was that the entire building was being converted into one massive home: no doubt for one very rich couple or a very rich family of ten, since the three-story brownstone could easily hold ten bedrooms and five bathrooms. From her floor, she could see straight into the top floor of the building, where she saw a spacious living room with dark-stained pine floors and had a full view of the expansive rooftop deck: covered in wood, complete with a built-in fire pit and benches. Last week, gardeners had arrived with potted plants, and so the entire deck was in bloom with white and yellow flowers.

Now she studied the movers. None of them looked

up. Chloe had gotten used to not being seen from her vantage point. People just didn't glance up beyond the second floor of her building. Chloe sank into the little bench at her bay window, sipping her soda and watching the men work. Because it was so hot, Chloe could only bear to wear a tank top with thin straps and a pair of old gym shorts. She hadn't bothered putting on makeup, because she worked from home and the humidity would just melt it off anyway. She'd swept her dark, nearly black hair up in a hastily made ponytail, but didn't care. She doubted the movers would be looking up. She felt invisible on her perch. She took another sip, watching the burly workers below as they waited to unload their cargo. They seemed not able to get in.

Then a brand-new Maserati roared up to the back of the building, steered by a man in his early 30s. He parked in the alley, not caring about a proper parking space. She guessed a man with a Maserati could afford a parking ticket. He popped out of the driver's seat, dressed in a T-shirt and shorts. Hang on. *Hello.* Tall, built like a linebacker, with muscles she could see from where she sat. What was he—a boxer? A fitness trainer? No trainer she knew could afford a Maserati.

He ran a hand through a thick head of dirty-blond hair as he dropped his phone in his pocket. He instantly started directing the movers.

She glanced at his flat stomach hugged by his skintight shirt and thought: *Bet he's gay.* She didn't know any straight guys who worked that hard on their abs. And she knew next to no rich men who did. After all, why bother, when their wallets could speak for themselves?

But...if he is straight...mmm, mama. He had just the right amount of blond goatee covering his chin. She saw no ring on his left hand. Then he grabbed keys from his pocket and opened the back door. Could he be...the new neighbor? He certainly acted like it. And the Maserati fit the profile of someone who'd just bought a whole building for himself.

She willed him to look up, to see her, but he didn't. Not that he would.

No one bothers to see me up here. The benefits of being invisible meant that she could spy with abandon.

The new neighbor was gorgeous, with a capital *G*. And had more money than God if he was going to live in that building all by himself. Lincoln Park real estate was anything but cheap. Just ask Chance the Rapper, who lived two streets over. Not that money alone really spoke to Chloe. Sure, she wouldn't mind having more of it, but her Korean dad and Irish mom raised her with Midwestern values. They told her to work hard, keep her head down and not be flashy.

A strand of her nearly black hair fell into her face. She blew it off her sticky forehead and fumbled with her tank-top spaghetti strap that kept falling off her shoulder. She watched as the new neighbor directed the movers, as they unloaded the truck—a big gray sectional coming first, as they maneuvered it into the open door across the way.

At least I'm not moving a couch wearing a jump-suit in this heat, she thought, fanning herself and taking a sip of her now-lukewarm soda.

A few minutes later she saw them maneuver the same couch into the third-floor living room. She realized then she could see the entire living room, the fireplace, a bit of the kitchen and even, when the bedroom door was open, a little of that as well. And now the shades were up and she saw movers walking about the space below. She watched the new neighbor in the alley pick up a few boxes himself, his biceps rippling beneath the weight. What kind of billionaire *lifts his own boxes*? Now Chloe's curiosity was piqued. Maybe she was wrong. Maybe that wall of muscle was the billionaire's personal assistant? Yet something told her no. It was the way he carried himself. This man was in charge, and not just of the move.

The intriguing man disappeared into the staircase. Chloe's phone dinged then, an incoming message, an email alert. She absently went to get her phone, and scrolled through her messages. Spam, actually. She dismissed it and returned to the window, noticing that the mystery neighbor popped up at the top floor and walked the boxes into the living room. *Doesn't hurt to watch, does it? Not that they'll see me anyway.*

He hadn't noticed her, and yet she was close

enough to see his forehead start to glisten a little with sweat. For once, she was glad of her invisibility cloak. Now she could see his face a bit better as he stood at the window, looking down. He took off his sunglasses and wiped his forehead, and she could see his eyes weren't brown. Blue, maybe? Or green? Hard to tell. He swiped at the bead of sweat on his temple.

Wish I could wipe that off...with my tongue, she found herself thinking, and then giggled to herself at the ludicrous idea as she clutched her phone in her sweaty palm. Where did that come from? It had to be because she was newly single, she figured. Suddenly, everybody was a possibility. As she finished off her can of soda, she watched the new neighbor dump a box in the living room and then run an arm across his own sweaty brow. Then, to her utter surprise, he whipped off his tee.

Oh...my. Hello there, sexy. She hadn't seen such an amazing chest before except on the giant posters of her gym. He had abs, yes, and that amazing little vee stretching down into his low-slung khakis. His well-defined pecs and chiseled arms seemed like they should be wielding a hammer.

She also noticed this bad boy had tattoos. A big one across his right arm and shoulder. What was it? She couldn't make it out. She pulled up her phone's camera and then zoomed in, trying to get a better look. Was the tattoo part of a wing? She wasn't sure.

Okay, what bazillionaire lifted his own boxes *and*

had tattoos? Chloe shook her head. The new neighbor was all kinds of mystery rolled into some serious eye candy. He patted his face with his own shirt, and Chloe felt like she'd suddenly been taken out of time. Everything she watched seemed to be on a slow-motion reel, even as her sexy new neighbor grabbed a bottle of water and took a deep swig. She watched his Adam's apple bob and suddenly wished he'd dump the whole bottle on his head.

What's wrong with you? This isn't a male revue, for goodness' sake. Chloe tried to mentally shake herself, but she still sat at the window anyway, transfixed. She clutched the phone in her hand. Should she take a picture? She was tempted. Then the dazzling neighbor moved away from the window and out of sight.

Dammit. Where did the bad boy with the abs go?

She pushed forward, trying to see, and her spaghetti strap slipped again from her shoulder. She wore no bra, since it was too hot for one in her opinion, and the fabric of her shirt slung dangerously low, but she didn't pay it any mind. She was too focused on getting one more glimpse of her Nordic god neighbor.

Where had he gone? She couldn't see him at the windows anymore. The door to the roof creaked open then, and she saw him head out on the slate tile of the patio. Now he was even closer, a perfect place to take a picture. Should she? Her friends would never believe such a hunky man had moved in. And what if he was famous? An actor, maybe? From *Chicago Fire* or one of the dozens of regular shows that filmed in downtown Chicago?

She held up her phone, debating whether to take a shot, when he suddenly glanced up and their eyes met. For a second, she froze from sheer shock. Surely he wasn't *actually seeing her*. Nobody saw her up here. But he gave a slight nod of his head, a little smile, and she realized he had seen her. He held his hand up in a wave.

Horrified, Chloe scrambled to hide her phone, but the sudden movement sent the smartphone slipping out of her sweaty grasp. She watched helplessly as her phone—brand-new—toppled out of her open window. She leaned out of the window, but it was too late. Her prized possession was taken by gravity. It flipped downward to the alley below, missing his shiny new Maserati by inches, landing between it and the moving truck with a sickening crack on the asphalt.

She glanced back up at the neighbor, who seemed surprised, but was watching her—not the phone. He was transfixed, frozen, and that was when she realized—too late—she was hanging out of her window, practically falling out of her tank top, the fabric so low she was flashing the man her nipples.

Chloe, mortified, pulled up her shirt, ducked away from her window and retreated to her kitchen, her heart pounding.

That's just great. Throw your phone out the win-

*dow. Flash the neighbor. Maybe he'll throw you
some Mardi Gras beads.*

The heat of embarrassment burned her cheeks.
Maybe he's gay and doesn't care. At least, she could
hope for that. After a few minutes, Chloe felt like an
idiot standing barefoot in her kitchen. She wondered
if he was still there. Carefully, she tiptoed from her
kitchen, and then kicked herself. *He can't hear me,*
she scolded, and tried to catch a glimpse far from
her window. But when she looked out, she didn't see
the bad boy anymore. She slunk closer to the window, trying to hide herself behind a side curtain.
Nope. The deck below her sat empty except for the
potted plants.

Then she remembered her phone, dropped four
stories onto the ground below. She needed that—it
was her lifeline!

She didn't have time to change. What if someone
stepped on it? What if someone stole it? She roused
herself out of her stupor and moved to her front door.
She jammed her feet into flip-flops and headed for
the staircase. She swung open the back door ready
to jump into the alley and nearly collided with…her
new neighbor.

He was holding her mangled and decidedly
cracked phone in his hand. "Uh… I think you
dropped this?"

Standing in front of him, she realized now how
very tall he was. His muscled shoulders were all
power. And he still wasn't wearing a shirt. And she

was more than aware of the fact that she wasn't wearing a bra.

"Uh… Yeah. I…" *I just flashed you a second ago. Sorry about that.* "Uh… Thanks." She grabbed the phone, with its shattered face and bent corner. It still lit up when she touched it. That was good, at least.

"I'm… Jackson Drake." He extended a strong hand.

She took his hand dumbly and shook it. His palm was smooth and big. The man had big hands, bear paws almost. What was it that they said about big hands? His sharp blue eyes never left her.

"Looks like we'll be neighbors." A slow smile curved his lips. He had nice teeth, too. Model-white.

So he *did* own that whole building. What was a billionaire doing…fetching her phone? She happened to glance at his wrist and saw the gleaming Rolex there. Yep, definitely rich.

"And you are…?"

Idiot. Didn't even tell him your name. "Chloe… Chloe Park."

"Nice to meet you, Chloe. Do you mind if I call you by your first name? I feel like after today, we need to be on a first-name basis." He grinned a sly, wolfish smile.

Still, her face flamed at the reference of her spilling out of her shirt. "I'm sorry. I'm not used to having neighbors. I'm not even in the habit of shutting my blinds. That building has been abandoned for so long."

"Don't change on my account." He took a slight

step closer. His bare chest filled up most of her field of vision. She wondered if his skin felt as smooth as it looked. Something told her he wasn't gay. Gay men didn't flirt like this with her.

Chloe again lost the ability to speak. Pretty soon, he'd start thinking she was slow. Chloe felt a tingle at the back of her knees. "Park…" he said, blue eyes never leaving hers. "Is that Korean?"

"Dad's Korean. Mom's Irish. You know, a living representation of the melting pot. They live in Seattle, but I see them a couple of times a year…" What was she yammering on about? She always did that when she was nervous.

"Hey! Drake!" called one of the movers carrying a large box. "This going to the first floor or…?"

Jackson hesitated, seeming to want to linger. Or maybe that was just because he didn't want to deal with moving. Moving day was always terrible, no matter how rich you were, Chloe supposed.

"Well, I see you're busy, but, uh…thanks for the phone. It's my lifeline." She held up her battered phone. *If* her lifeline still worked, that is.

Jackson nodded. He couldn't be more confident in his own skin, standing at her back alley door. But then, why wouldn't he be? He was gorgeous and rich. He was probably used to women falling at his feet. *Or falling out of their tops*, she thought ruefully.

"Until…next time then. Chloe." He nodded once at her, and she was held there, for a second, trapped in his ice-blue eyes. Eventually, she remembered she was a sweaty, unshowered mess and wasn't wearing a stitch of makeup—or a bra. Her girls were probably bouncing all over the place. Self-consciousness consumed her. She crossed her arms awkwardly across her chest.

"Till next time," she squeaked, like a mouse, and retreated. Even as the alley door closed, she felt her heart pounding.

CHAPTER TWO

JACKSON DRAKE COULDN'T get his mind off the dark-haired beauty who'd given him a show as he drove his Maserati down North Avenue later that day. He grinned to himself. He remembered her shock and embarrassment when she'd realized she'd shown him her left breast and almost all of the right, her dark nipples puckered just the way he liked them. They came in the perfect size, natural, but not too heavy, much more than a handful. He wondered what they'd feel like against his palms. The idea of having a sexy new neighbor who often went braless was a perk he hadn't anticipated when he'd bought the old icehouse. Drake had made a fortune in real estate, in transforming old buildings into new condos and offices. He was one of the city's most successful large-scale flippers. A real estate magazine had labeled him a renegade, since he always bet on buildings and neighborhoods others wrote off, plus, his bad-boy look made him seem more biker gang than Fortune 500. But his facial hair grew so fast, he'd need to shave twice a day if he had even a fighting chance of being clean shaven, so he decided long ago not to fight it. Goatees and beards came easy to him.

But those who thought he looked more thug than businessman would be wrong. He prided himself on doing more research, knowing everything there was to know about a neighborhood, before he invested in it. But somehow he'd missed the intel on the sexy neighbor next door.

I would've finished the renovations earlier if I'd known, he mused, grinning. *And maybe added more windows.* He was already regretting only having one on the second floor facing the alley.

The light turned green and he gunned his car, beating the BMW in the lane next to him as he roared down the street.

He thought about her cracked phone and frowned. He made a mental note: he'd grab one of the many smartphones they kept at the office to hand out to new Realtors. It would be easy enough to replace, and besides, he was just being neighborly. He imagined what she'd do when she saw the new phone. Would her face light up with delight?

Then, almost instantly, his excitement faded a tad. He'd wondered, briefly, if it had all been an act. Most women saw the money before they saw him. He worked hard on his body, but he'd begun to think that didn't matter in the least. Hell, if some woman wanted him for his abs it would be a welcome change of pace. Most women saw the Maserati and Rolex, and then didn't care what he looked like. Jackson shook his head. It was why he'd all but given up hope on finding someone who actually cared about *him*. His last relationship had been a disaster from the get-go: she'd been a social climber disguised as a bartender—Laurie, a woman he'd caught in his bathroom, legs up on the bathroom counter, as she tried to tip the contents of a used condom inside her to impregnate herself. It was a calculated move to get child support, or 20 percent of his gross income per year until the baby turned eighteen.

Every time Jackson thought he'd become as cynical as you could be about women, he managed to find a new level. The experience had been enough to make him want to never date again. Lately, Jackson had been relying on old friends-with-benefits relationships, the kind that came with no strings, no commitments. Women who liked nice meals out, the occasional gift, and didn't mind that Jackson would disappear for months at a time. Having money wasn't all bad.

He'd been telling himself for years that this was exactly what he wanted: a rotation of gorgeous and willing women. Mostly, this worked just fine, until he spent Thanksgiving with his cousin and his wife and kids in the burbs and wondered what it would be like to have a family of his own: a house full of love and laughter and a little bit of chaos. It was really why Laurie's antics had hurt him so much. He worried that he'd never find genuine love, a woman who could see beyond the money and could love the man beneath.

He steered his car to the office bearing his name—Drake Properties—and pulled into the underground parking beneath the sleek skyscraper that housed his office in the Gold Coast near downtown Chicago, aptly named for its stunning multimillion-dollar condos and its proximity to the Magnificent Mile, home to the swankiest stores in the city. He was happy to see that most of the spaces dedicated to his office were empty. That was a good thing. That meant Realtors were out doing their jobs. After all, you couldn't sell property from inside an air-conditioned office. He headed to the elevator, texting his assistant to let him know he'd be arriving soon. In seconds he was inside the lobby of the building, which they shared with a few other businesses. He waved at the security guard up front and then headed to the bank of elevators that would take him to the top floor.

The elevator door barely opened before his assistant, Hailey, greeted him with a piping-hot cappuccino, foamed up just the way he liked it, an elaborate swirled pattern down the center.

"Good morning, sir," Hailey said, beaming her million-dollar smile as she handed him the perfectly foamed cappuccino. Blond perfection in a steel-gray pencil skirt and blouse, Hailey was all business, just the way he liked it. Clients were stunned by her beauty, but he loved the fact that she never missed the smallest detail.

"Here are the dailies," she said, handing him a folder with the highlights of the day as well, including the brewing deals in the office. "And the Housing Network called again. They wanted to know if you'd given any more thought to their show." Hailey paused at his door, waiting for his answer.

Jackson shook his head. "Don't have time for reality TV discussions this week," he said, even though he knew HN wouldn't give up. They'd been hounding him for months to come do a guest spot on their show that put experts in touch with amateur home flippers. While the possibility was intriguing, Jackson had his hands full with current projects, and fame had never really interested him much.

"Thank you, Hailey."

"Yes, sir," Hailey said. "Oh, one more thing. Mr. Roberts is waiting for you. In the lobby."

"Why?" Jackson frowned. Roberts was his major competition in Chicago, and the only other developer who flipped buildings as fast as Jackson did. But while Jackson believed in revamping the community and trying to keep housing reasonably affordable, caring about the city as a whole, Roberts was a typical slumlord: he'd been born wealthy, a trust fund baby who had gotten richer on the backs of the poor. He had a vast holding of decrepit properties on the South Side. The two never saw eye to eye on anything. So why was he waiting for a meeting?

"He would only tell me that you'd want to hear his proposition."

"I'm not interested in any deal that man offers." Jackson took a sip of his cappuccino and then headed into his spacious corner office, made almost completely of glass. His sleek glass-legged desk waited for him, as did his new laptop. From his vantage point, he could see Lake Michigan, dotted with small white sailboats, the beaches nearby filled with sunbathers, even on a weekday.

Hailey barely hid a smile. "That's what I figured. Shall I tell him to leave?"

"No need, Miss Hailey," came a baritone from Jackson's office door. The two turned to see Kent Roberts standing there. Jackson frowned. He glanced at the tall, fit, dark-haired real estate baron hanging in his office door and hated the look of him: the preppy blue blazer, crisp khakis, expensive loafers and gleaming designer aviators perched on top of his wavy dark hair. His preppy, too-buttoned-up style rubbed Jackson the wrong way. It was as if he'd never grown out of the exclusive prep school uniform look. Then again, he probably went to boarding schools as a kid, so maybe he didn't know how else to dress.

Jackson was a man who liked to get his hands dirty, who would be just as likely to pick up a hammer on a construction site as blueprints. Kent, however, had delicate, manicured hands that had never seen a day's hard work in his whole life. The two were polar opposites.

"Sir?" Hailey asked, her single word loaded with meaning.

"It's all right, Hailey. I'll handle this."

With a swift nod, she backed out of his office, leaving him and Roberts alone.

Jackson ran a hand over his goatee, which was quickly on the border of turning into a full-fledged beard. He took smug satisfaction in Kent's baby-faced chin. The man couldn't grow anything, he was pretty sure. Jackson sneezed and had a moustache.

"What can I do for you?" Jackson braced himself. He'd learned long ago not to underestimate his adversary. He might look like he never got his hands dirty, but he wasn't afraid to stab anybody in the back.

"It's what I can do for *you*, friend." Kent smiled, but the smile didn't quite reach his eyes. "I heard you moved into your house on MacKenzie. We're neighbors."

"Neighbors?" Jackson asked stiffly.

"Well, I just bought the property next door."

Jackson frowned. How did he not know the building was for sale? He would've scooped it up, if only to protect his property values. Kent grinned, knowing he'd won that small victory.

"Which one?" Jackson asked.

"1209."

That was when Jackson realized it was Chloe's building, his sexy new neighbor. Now it really didn't sit well with him. He didn't like the idea of Chloe having a new slumlord owning her lease, a man who'd no doubt raise her rent but then refuse to fix anything. He might not know Chloe well, but what he did know he liked, and besides, no one deserved that.

"What do you plan to do with it?" Jackson asked.

Kent grinned even bigger. "Why, sell it to you, of course."

Now Jackson was on full alert. Kent was not the kind of man to ever do him any favors. "Why?"

"Because I know you'll make me the best offer. You've got all that *new* money lying around." He tapped Jackson's desk to make sure he hadn't missed the dig. "I'm sure you can afford it. Unless…you'd rather save your money for NASCAR, or whatever it is you like."

Kent always made a point of referencing the fact that Jackson came from humble beginnings. Kent had inherited his wealth. Never really worked a day in his life. Jackson's father worked as a carpenter. He just happened to have a heart attack on the job when he was near retirement, and that gave Jackson the ability to buy his first office and flip it. Sure, they'd both inherited money, but Jackson's inheritance came with much fewer zeros.

"I earned my money," he said. "I'm not embarrassed about that."

Kent frowned. "Well, like I said, I think you should think long and hard about making me a good offer." Jackson suddenly felt that if he didn't buy the building, Kent might turn it into something terrible, like a truck stop in the middle of the city. Or a strip club. Something that would make living next door impossible. "How about I have my people get in touch with your people… I just know we can make a deal."

Kent stood, arms crossed, a fixed grin on his face that said he was enjoying this little meeting a little too much. Kent loved lording this over Jackson. He had no doubt the developer would insist on the most unreasonable price for the building, just so Jackson would keep it out of his hands. Honestly, it was lazy and stalkerish of Kent. Was his plan just to follow Jackson around the city? Buy up anything next door?

Jackson sighed. "Fine," he said, hating this little game of cat and mouse. He'd rather just ignore Kent, pretend he didn't exist, but Kent had other ideas. He'd seemed obsessed lately with picking a fight, and it was in no small part due to the fact that Jackson was far more successful than Kent, had reality TV offers when Kent had none, and had outbid him on a recent parkland deal with the city, a lucrative project that would turn junkyards into public spaces. Jackson understood that Kent was a bad developer, that he'd lost out on a number of big deals recently because he hadn't had the vision or the courage to jump into new projects. Jackson had both. Of course, if Kent spent less time in strip clubs and more time reading up on real estate, he could be as successful, too.

Kent hung around, standing near the door, that smug grin on his face that Jackson hated. Jackson glanced back at his computer, dismissal obvious. When Kent didn't leave right away, Jackson reluctantly looked up. "Is there anything else?"

"I'll have my people call your people," he said, completely unaware of how pretentious and clichéd he sounded.

Jackson didn't respond, but stared at his computer screen until Kent had left.

Hailey rushed in when he was gone.

"Everything…okay?" she asked, tentative.

"Fine. He's just blowing hot air—as usual. The man has an endless supply." Jackson shook his head.

"How bad is this rivalry going to get?" Hailey asked. "Should I schedule a fight after school?" Her mouth quirked up in a teasing smile. Hailey, who just married her longtime partner, Kristi, last year, had little tolerance for testosterone-fueled fights.

"I would totally win that fight," he felt the need to say, for the record.

"Oh, I know you would, sir." Hailey grinned.

"You'll be hearing from him about a property near my house. I'm sure the first offer will be laughable. Just be on the lookout."

"Will do," Hailey said and ducked out of his office once more.

He took another sip of his now-lukewarm cappuccino and tapped on his keyboard, bringing his computer screen to life. After discussions with Kent, he needed to cleanse his palate. He thought about his new neighbor and her dark eyes and…exposed nipple. He loved her look, not quite Korean, not quite Irish, something in between. He was all kinds of mutt, mostly Celtic, a little bit Cherokee in there somewhere, Ger-

man, and a spattering of Cajun, too. Curious about
Chloe, he pulled up her building and saw it was a
rental property, apartments, which he knew already.
He saw old pictures of what must be her condo, a small
efficiency. As he swiped through them, his phone lit
up with an incoming message from his ex-girlfriend.

Miss you.

He stared at the message and shook his head. Laurie. Really? She missed him? He knew that was a lie.
She missed his money, maybe. Him? No way. He
deleted the message. Hearing from Laurie felt like
a bucket of cold water over his head. Why was he
thinking about the mystery girl next door? She was
probably no different than Laurie.

Even Jackson realized he was slipping down into
a dark place. He didn't like it, either. Didn't like his
new morose attitude. He'd always been a go-getter.
That was how he'd built his empire from nothing.

Then he got another message. How's the move
going? Bed assembled yet? This from Annaliese,
one of his friends with benefits, an Eastern Euro-
pean model who was more than happy to be kept
in rotation.

Maybe, he said.

If it is, how about I come over and help you break
it in tonight?

Jackson thought about Annaliese's curves, her

sleek red hair and the way she had a knack for distracting him from problems, namely with her talented hands. And mouth.

He'd never fall in love Annaliese—she was far too single-minded for him, and it was purely just about the sex. She never wanted dinner or drinks. She'd made it clear from the start that she had no interest in any relationship, and even if she did, he'd be the last person she'd think about marrying. Annaliese had a theory that no one could be faithful, really, especially rich men. Not that she'd given him the chance. Still, he couldn't even imagine what it would be like to sit across from Annaliese at a dinner table. Most of the time when she showed up at his place, she wore a raincoat and nothing else. Occasionally, she'd wear garters. Or transparent lace. Or thongs. He found himself wondering what she'd choose tonight.

It's a date, he wrote.

You know I don't date, she wrote back, and he grinned.

CHAPTER THREE

"YOU SHOULD COME out with us tonight," said Ryan on the phone as Chloe glanced down at her just-microwaved burrito. She had her hands-free set tucked in her ear as she sat in her warm kitchen, though it was cooling off now that the sun had set outside and a soothing breeze seeped into her open window. She glanced at her shattered screen. The phone still worked as a phone, but there was no way she'd be able to check text messages or Twitter. It would be one more expense she'd need to make when she got her next check. She'd just have to wait until then. It didn't help that most of her social media clients of late were nonprofits who took a long time paying their bills. She'd worked most of the afternoon with a nonprofit group called Our Home, which tried to help low-income families stay in neighborhoods that were slowly being gentrified.

She'd uploaded some photos of their work. Much of what they did resembled Habitat for Humanity projects, except they repaired damaged buildings and pressured local aldermen not to green-light commercial real estate that could threaten low-income housing. Of course, if Chloe didn't get paid soon, she'd have to move herself to the category of *low income*. Her laptop remained open on the dining room table, proof she had been working some today. She was still wearing the outfit she'd flashed her new neighbor in (her pajama tank and shorts, having not bothered to change since she'd been chained to her laptop most of the day). Owning her own consulting business meant she got to work from home, but it also meant that work never stopped, either. Not if she wanted her business to survive. She'd just gotten a notice in her mailbox, too, something about a new owner of the building. She hoped that didn't mean a rent hike when her lease was up in a few months, but she knew it might.

"Ryan, I don't know…" *I'd have to shower. Change. It seems like such a production.* Or she could sit and eat her burrito, binge-watch *Game of Thrones*, and call it a night. The latter seemed so much simpler.

"Brendan says if you don't get out of the house *once* this week, we're officially holding an intervention." Chloe grinned. She loved Ryan and Brendan— she'd stood up in their wedding the summer before. She'd been friends with Ryan since college and had been thrilled when he'd met Brendan—the two were great together: both dark-haired and lean, both rabid outdoorsmen, with a bent toward mountain climbing. Whenever Chloe thought love might not be in the cards for her, she looked at them and thought that if they could find their soul mates, then probably so could she. She would've been nauseated by their sickly sweet Facebook posts, except that she loved them both to death.

"Seriously, Chlo, how many days in a row have you worn the outfit you're wearing *right now*?"

"One," she said. Then she wondered if that was true. Had she changed yesterday? Now she couldn't quite remember, though she had to admit, the thought had crossed her mind to just head to bed in the same pajamas. Would that be a new low? Not showering and not changing two days in a row. Hell, but wasn't this one of the major perks of working at home?

"I think you're lying."

Chloe had to laugh. "I'll catch you guys next time, okay?"

Ryan sighed. "Okay, but you're starting to turn into some weird hermit, you know that? You need to get out. Socialize with people. You do *social media* all day, but you *never talk to anyone anymore*. Like when was your last *human* interaction?"

"That's not necessary for my job," she pointed out.

"No, but it is for your mental health. Since the breakup…"

"Don't even mention his name." Kevin. The investment banker who'd made fun of her consulting business, who often told her she should "get a real job" and endlessly made jokes about how work done in her pajamas was no work at all. But Chloe was proud of her accomplishments, proud of being her own boss. But because she didn't have a traditional job, Kevin thought she was somehow less important. He saw a girlfriend mostly as an accessory and not a person, which was why he called her by the wrong name in bed…a name she discovered from a series of lurid text messages on his phone belonged to his co-worker, a woman he'd been sleeping with on the side.

"You've been hiding, Chlo. Time to break free and get out there," Ryan said.

She knew he was right, but she didn't feel like getting out there. As awful as Kevin had been to her, she'd gotten to the point where she had really started to think they might get married. He'd told her as much. The fact that he'd been cheating was a blow she still felt six months later. It was because Chloe knew she wanted more. She was closing in on thirty, and her biological clock had kicked into overdrive. She wanted a baby, a family, a husband, and she was pretty sure she wasn't going to find any of those things going out to a bar with Ryan.

"I will—eventually," she said, and glanced at her cooling burrito on her plate, thinking about how un-appetizing it looked. "I just need some time. Besides, I've got a new neighbor who just moved in. Totally ripped. And loaded, too."

"Oh! A Christian Grey!"

"Uh…well, if Christian Grey wore shorts and had tattoos." She took a bite of the burrito and nearly

scalded her tongue. She dropped the too-hot micro-
waved dinner.

"Ooooh. A bad boy. A *rich* bad boy. I like it."

Chloe laughed. "Don't tell Brendan. He'll get jealous."

"He might. You should go for that. Ride that *bike*
if you know what I mean."

"I think he might be gay. I mean, he's got a six-
pack." Chloe bit her lip as she wandered to her window and glanced at her new neighbor's darkened
third floor. She'd watched all afternoon but hadn't
seen Jackson again. Instead, an army of assistants
had come and unpacked him entirely. She'd never
seen such efficiency before, but in a matter of hours,
they'd unpacked his kitchen, set up his bed, even
hung art on the walls. It must be nice to be rich,
she'd thought, as she'd watched his minions do all
the grunt work.

Ryan considered this. "You're right. Six-pack
abs—they are rampant in the gay community," he
deadpanned.

Just then, the neighbor's light flickered on. Chloe
backed away from her window. "Uh…gotta go,
okay? I'll call you later."

"Just remember what I said. Don't be a hermit!"

"Love you!" she called, and then clicked off. She
told herself she shouldn't spy on her neighbor, and
besides, it was probably one of his assistants anyway.
But as she hovered near the curtains, she watched
Jackson enter the third floor from the open stair-

way at the back of the living room. He immediately tugged off his shirt.

Oh, my. That was a view she could get used to: well-toned pecs, rippled abs, broad, muscled shoulders. She wondered again what he did for a living. Model? Action hero? Jackson could be either. He disappeared into the far right room, his bedroom, as she'd watched his home-decor minions set up his bed, and carry in armful after armful of expensive suits. She didn't see a kitchen, so it had to be on one of the two floors below. She couldn't imagine what, exactly, he was doing with all that space. For all she knew, the first floor could be an indoor basketball court. Or filled with trampolines. She had no idea how the über-rich lived.

Maybe he was just going to bed, she thought, and then went back to her burrito. She took a bite that was still part frozen. How was one end on fire and the other an ice cube? Ugh. She put it down, suddenly not feeling like eating it. She clicked off the overhead kitchen light, the oven light the only thing illuminating her small kitchen. She glanced up and saw Jackson emerging from his bedroom wearing only mesh shorts, slung low on his hips, and still no shirt. He sank down on his plush leather couch and put his feet up. His phone must've sounded because he picked it up and pressed it to his ear. Then, a second later, he tapped the screen. He laid back on the couch, his eyes on the staircase. Suddenly, a woman clad only in the shortest silk jumper Chloe had ever seen appeared on the stairwell in strappy stiletto heels and too much makeup, her auburn bob cut at chin length. She was gorgeous. She sauntered over to the couch, a pouty expression on her face, and he sat there, watching her.

Was that his girlfriend? She felt a hardened pit at the center of her stomach.

But she didn't greet him like a girlfriend. They didn't hug or kiss. Instead, she began to slip out of her little shorts romper, the silk sleeves fluttering downward, revealing the fact that she wore no bra. She was all business, this one. No warm fuzzies. He watched the show appreciatively as she kicked out of the one-piece, now wearing only stilettos, her bare, toned body in front of him.

Well, he's definitely not gay.

Chloe knew she needed to stop watching. But she couldn't. She clutched at the curtain, half-hidden, mesmerized by the action unfolding in front of her. It was a billion times more interesting than her abandoned burrito. Her bad-boy neighbor stood then, and the woman knelt in front of him. She jerked down his shorts as he grabbed a handful of her hair and gave it a playful tug.

I can't watch this, her mind screamed, and yet she couldn't look away. The woman freed him, and Chloe nearly gasped...he was bigger than Kevin. Much bigger. She didn't even know they *came* that big, even while the woman worked at it with both hands, and he stiffened beneath her touch. He watched her intently as she took part of him in her mouth, the tip. *God, did they not know the windows were wide-open? Did they not know she could see...everything?*

This was taking the invisible fourth floor to an *entirely* different level.

Yet part of her realized neither one of them cared. They were intent on sex, only on the sex. After a minute, he pulled her to her feet and whirled her around, completely in command as he bent her across the arm of his couch. Jackson reached his fingers down to her inner thigh, stroking her, then disappearing inside her. She moaned, throwing her head back. Then he had a condom package in his mouth and ripped it open, rolling the latex down his now-ready self. Then he entered her: strong, possessive, decisive.

I shouldn't watch this. Yet she couldn't turn away, either.

Chloe felt her whole body run hot. For a second, she imagined herself there, over that couch, him taking her from behind like an animal, him filling her up. She watched his abs tighten as he worked himself in and out, the woman's face showing joy and want, as she took the whole thick length of him again and again. Chloe watched, transfixed, unable to turn away. She'd never had a man that big before. What would that feel like? The strange woman in his living room gripped the sofa cushions, her knuckles white as she seemed to cry out. Was she climaxing? Her whole body vibrated...and Chloe shivered. God, she felt a stab of jealousy. She wanted to climax just like that, feeling Jackson deep inside her.

Instantly, her body came alive, her belly feeling warm and tingling, her pajama shorts suddenly sticky between her legs. *What am I doing? I'm a Peeping Tom. It's wrong...* And yet all she wanted to do was slip her hands down the waistband of her own shorts, to touch herself. She could feel a beat of a pulse between her legs, feel the want there, the need.

Wasn't this illegal? Snooping in people's windows?

I need to turn away. Close my blinds. But she kept watching, mesmerized and focusing on his magnificent body, his strong hands holding her hips, as he explored her deepest places. Her nipples stood at attention, her small, firm breasts bouncing with his every move. She rocked against him, too, grinding upward, arching her back, enjoying every inch of him.

Chloe bit her lip, feeling her nipples strain against her own shirt, and suddenly her body was overcome by want, like a fever. She wanted to be on the other side of that glass window. She wanted to feel the man's hands on her. Those thoughts consumed her as she stood half-hidden by her curtain.

She was almost tempted to touch herself then, scratch the itch building deep within her. But no. That would be wrong. Wouldn't it?

Chloe watched him, his eyes on the woman's

body, his face serious. Then, as if he could sense her watching, he glanced up, and for a heart-stopping second, he saw her.

She froze. Ice-cold fear ran down her spine. He saw her! She'd been caught spying!

Yet she couldn't break his gaze, his blue-eyed stare. Her heart pounded in her chest. She was caught.

He's going to be mad. He could even call the police...

Then, the smallest hint of a smile quirked his lip. He almost looked...amused. He kept eye contact with her and he thrust even deeper into his prize.

Her mouth dropped open. His gaze felt like a tractor beam, holding her in place. He gave her the littlest of nods. *Go on*, his eyes seemed to dare her, *watch me.* The woman before him had her eyes closed, obviously enjoying the feel of him inside her, but suddenly it didn't even matter he was having sex with another woman. As Jackson watched Chloe, it felt like the two of them were the only people in the world. It felt strangely intimate, somehow. Chloe was watching the man at his most vulnerable, and Jackson was letting her.

Something about that was so wrong...so naughty... yet she couldn't break his gaze, couldn't turn from the window. How could he watch her when he was inside someone else? And yet, he seemed to...*want* her to watch.

Could that be?

And was it her imagination or was he turned on

by it? Yes, she realized. He was. Excited by her. By *her* watching. She felt strangely powerful then. She wasn't a third wheel; she was *affecting* what she saw.

He leaned over, nuzzling the woman's neck and cupping her firm breast, tweaking the woman's pink nipple, but his eyes never left hers all the while, as if somehow, he was offering to do this to her. Heat burned in her belly.

Yes. Just like that. Touch her.

Touch me.

Instinctively, Chloe's hand covered her own breast as she felt her desire grow. The weight of her own hand against her chest felt like his then. She imagined what it would feel like for him to nuzzle her neck, even as he pushed ever deeper inside her.

Jackson straightened again, grabbing the woman's hips, moving her slightly so she could see him from the side, see the very thick length of him move in... and out. God, he was huge, so hard for her. How did she even take that much?

Yes, Jackson. Just like that, she thought. *That's how I'd want it.*

Fast.

Hard.

Deep.

He picked up his pace, as if he could hear her own thoughts. He was all animal, all want. Slickness ran between her legs as she gawked, unable—and unwilling—to look away. All the while, he stared up at her, sharp blue eyes never leaving her face.

She wanted to see him come, wanted to see him pour himself into this woman, because that was what she'd want. All of him. All that he could give her.

Then, after several furious thrusts, he came: his face overcome with the pleasure of pure relief. Jackson briefly closed his eyes as he'd found his release. She knew then she'd helped him. She'd excited him, pushed him over the edge. She felt the thudding pulse between her own legs and knew he'd had the same effect on her. Her body had come alive with need and want, as both flooded the blood in her veins, pumped by her fast-beating heart. What she'd give at that moment to be able to feel him inside her. God, she wanted him.

Then the woman before him opened her eyes, and the spell was broken. Suddenly, the intimate little bubble she'd occupied with Jackson was burst. Chloe ducked behind her curtains, fearful the woman would see. She pressed her back against the brick wall, heart pounding in her ears.

What had just happened?

It was wrong what had just happened. So very wrong. How would she feel if someone had watched her and her…boyfriend? Yet she'd never been that brazen. She would've never done it with the blinds up like that. She remembered the confident smirk of the woman as she'd stepped out of her jumper. Chloe doubted the woman would even care if she'd been seen. Hell, she was the one who had sex in front of the windows at night, with the blinds up.

She clicked off her foyer light, her own apartment now dark. She felt the cloak of darkness like a cover of protection. Could she ever even look at Jackson again? She frantically shut her own curtains.

No. It had been wrong. She shouldn't have watched. Yet she liked it. She liked it even more when he'd caught her watching. When he'd shown her how much he'd enjoyed it. Those stark blue eyes watching her, excited by her watching... She'd never forget the look on his face when he'd come.

Heat built between her legs as she slipped her hand down the waistband of her shorts. She found herself so very wet, so very wanting. She touched her most delicate center and shivered, knowing this was what she'd badly wanted to do while she watched Jackson, and now she could hold back no longer. She thought about his hands, his eyes, how he'd feel inside her, filling her...and then, before she knew it, Chloe came in a heated rush, so fast, so hard, a quick explosion of need.

God, she'd never done that before: made herself come in just a matter of seconds. But she knew why this time had been different. It had been Jackson. All Jackson.

What would he do if he knew she'd...just done this? For him?

The thought danced in her mind. So wrong. Yet right.

She felt like she'd *been* there with him. And…her. Her heart settled a bit, her breathing slowed, and she wondered if her neighbor had gotten dressed. If he and that woman were cuddling, kissing now. The thought made her feel a flare of jealousy. Why? *I'm not his girlfriend. I'm just the neighbor who flashed him…and watched him come.* How she wished she could see that look of pure pleasure on his face again, but this time, with him deep, deep inside her.

She slumped down at her kitchen table and stared at her drawn curtains. Should she take another peek? Would she dare? No. She fought herself. *I've invaded the man's privacy enough. I've broken enough laws.*

What if Jackson called the police?

She shook her head. No. She remembered the pleasure on his face as he glanced up and saw her. No. He liked it. He liked it when she watched.

But who was that woman? Girlfriend? Escort? She wasn't sure which would be worse. She didn't like the idea of him having a girlfriend, an intimate, loving relationship, but she also didn't like the idea of him paying for sex, either. She heard a door slam in the alley and curiosity got the better of her. She jostled the curtain a centimeter and peered down. The woman he'd just had sex with slipped into an Uber waiting in the alley.

Definitely not a girlfriend, she thought. Then… what?

Chloe thought about the man in his big three-story building all by himself, sated now, maybe even still naked. Maybe rinsing off in the shower. For a split second, a crazy thought ran through her head…what if I went over? Rang his doorbell?

Instantly, she dismissed the thought. Really? She was going to…what? Tell him she was sorry for spying? Or ask him to do *exactly* what he'd just done to that woman to her?

Her inner thighs tingled at the thought. Heat rose in her abdomen again. She'd only just taken care of that. Hadn't she? Yet, was she wanting this again? So soon? Just the thought of seeing Jackson made her wet.

No. He'd think she was crazy. Wouldn't he?

After she watched the Uber drive away, she glanced back up at the new neighbor's windows. She didn't see him, and figured he'd moved to his room, though his blinds were still wide-open. Maybe he'd forget about the whole thing. Maybe he'd pretend it never happened. Maybe that was what she should do as well.

Then she saw him return with a bar of white soap in his hand and a small bowl of water. What was he…? She hid once more as he came to the windows. The idea of him seeing her spying *more* made her face flame with embarrassment. She waited for a few minutes, breathing hard.

Go to bed, Chloe, she told herself. *What are you even doing?*

She waited a few more moments that felt like hours. Should she look? Once more? What *was* he doing with that bar of soap?

Chloe peeked around the curtain, leaving just enough space for one eye. The living room was now empty. No sign of Jackson.

But he'd used the soap to write a message on his window. It was big enough for her to read.

Next time, want to do more than watch?

CHAPTER FOUR

CHLOE COULD BARELY sleep as she thought about what that message might mean. Did he want her to join him? Or join him *and* her? A threesome? Chloe thought about the woman's amazing body and instantly shelved that thought. No way could she get naked in the same room as that runway model. She wasn't about to let her muffin top compare to the skin-and-bones double-zero. Chloe had curves, and that meant that sometimes they jiggled when they weren't supposed to. Maybe Jackson hadn't really invited her over for sex. Maybe he was just calling her out on her snooping? She couldn't figure it out, no matter how hard she thought about it.

Part of her was embarrassed—after all, she'd watched her neighbor *have sex* and hadn't turned away. Granted, they'd left the windows open, but still. It violated basic rules of decency, and Chloe knew it, yet she couldn't help but feel even more intrigued by Jackson now that she knew he was so... endowed. Part of her wanted to tell him she *did* want to do more than watch. Ugh. Did that make her a raging slut? Probably. Or was she just looking after her own needs? Just *look* at the man! Gorgeous. Rich. Probably never intimidated in any locker room he ever entered. Chloe felt her face flush once more, the image of him naked flitting through her mind. Her running shoes pounded the pavement taking her east to the running trail on Lake Michigan.

After crossing a few intersections, she took the underground pedestrian tunnel to the lakefront and then wound her way north on the running trail, the sun rising above the pristine blue water, looking expansive across the horizon, so large it seemed impossible that it was fresh water and not the salty sea. The waves broke on the sandy beach as she ran, her heart thudding. The air got warmer while the sun rose in the sky and sweat broke out across her lower back. Just a few more feet, she thought to herself, and then she turned around, heading back to her apartment. This morning she'd shower. She'd put on something cute. Maybe even put on makeup.

Trying to impress Jackson? Hoping he gets a glimpse of you? Are you going to tell him he made you touch yourself last night?

Part of her wondered if he'd like to know.

She bit her lip. She'd taken the flirting to a new level when she'd watched him last night. She'd crossed a line. *And* that was probably his girlfriend. She couldn't get involved with a man who was so clearly involved and *deeply intimate with someone else*. She remembered just how deeply as she thought of his long, hard thrusts.

Though the woman hadn't stayed the night. That still didn't mean anything. There could be a million reasons for that. She was coveting her sexy neighbor, but he was in a relationship, and Chloe wasn't going to cross that line.

Was she? She bit her lip.

She ran back to her apartment, punching in the code to her place and trotting up the stairs and swiping the sweat off her forehead. She tried to catch her breath, convinced that the best thing to do was just ignore the message. Wasn't that the right thing? Yet, as she eyed the message—still in his window that morning—she felt a little shiver run down the back of her knees.

Next time, want to do more than watch?

Hell, yes, she thought to herself. She did. She wanted to do so much more than watch. Yet what was she thinking? Was she seriously going to *jump into bed with her neighbor*? What happened if she did and…the sex was terrible? Or worse, he broke things off? How would she feel living next door to an ex?

All rational thought told her that fooling around with her neighbor was a bad idea.

The cold water from the shower flushed a little of her desire down the drain, but her brain still buzzed with Jackson's invitation. She wanted to ask him a million questions, she needed to know exactly *what* he was offering.

She remembered the dark tattoos on his shoulder. Wings of some kind. She wanted to see them up close. To touch them. Read the inscription, if there was one. Ask him why he got them.

But he lives next door. This could be a disaster.

She thought about Ryan. He'd be telling her to go for it, no doubt. She almost imagined his hearty congratulations if she told him she'd finally found a rebound from Kevin. Hadn't Ryan just told her she needed to put Kevin behind her...and be more social?

Still, was she really going to do this?

Chloe hesitated. She still hadn't decided what to do about his message. Ignore it? Reply?

She glanced out her window, seeing the words there as clear as day, his third floor dark. Was he still sleeping? Had he left for work while she was out running?

She suddenly imagined herself writing a message on her window and then his blinds popping up, and him catching her in the act. The idea was mortifying. She wasn't even sure she could bear to look him in the eye after last night.

Chloe decided to ignore the message and booted up her computer. Then, after answering a few emails, she glanced once more at her neighbor's darkened windows. He might be at work. She might be able to send him a message. But what?

No. That was crazy. Why would she write him a message? *Just let it go, Chloe,* she told herself. *Just pretend none of it ever happened.*

Except that she couldn't. Even as she tried to focus on work, her attention kept wandering back to Jackson's darkened windows, to the message he left for her there. She couldn't forget his amazingly chiseled body, his blue eyes watching her.

She didn't have a bar of soap to write on her window, so opted for a pad of sticky notes. Her window was large, and she began laying out her message, using the notes to form letters. Then she stopped and ripped them all down. She glanced at Jackson's darkened windows. She was crazy for replying to this, wasn't she? She had to be crazy.

She glanced at the pink sticky notes in her hand. Maybe she was crazy. She started again before she lost her nerve.

Jackson sat at his desk in his office at Drake Properties, flipping a pen around his fingers, thinking about the dream he'd had the night before. He'd dreamed of Chloe, standing on the other side of a full glass window, wearing nothing but cherry-red heels. He hadn't been able to pay attention to even a single email this morning, as he wondered what Chloe had done when she saw his message that morning.

He knew he'd taken a risk putting the message on his window, but a man like him didn't build an empire without taking risks. He had seen the want on her face, knew that if he pushed hard—but not too hard—she might just wind up in his bed. How he wanted to know what she was like. Did she just like to watch? Or would she perform, too?

What was she doing right then? He hoped crafting

a response. The thought made him smile. He'd never been so aroused by a woman's eyes before. By her dark, sensual eyes. She'd watched him and Annaliese boldly, almost without fear. He couldn't wait to see what she'd be like in person, when there wasn't a window between them. He wanted to explore her darkest places.

"Mr. Drake? Call on line one. A Miss Smith?" his assistant asked through the intercom on his desk.

Jackson felt snapped back into reality. That was Laurie, his ex, on the line.

"Send her to voice mail, please," Jackson called to the intercom.

Just then, a new message popped up on his phone. From Laurie.

I need to talk to you. Please. Call me.

He hit Delete again, and then he thought about blocking her. She wasn't taking no for an answer, and it irked him.

There's nothing to talk about. We're done.

She quickly wrote back, But I love you.
Please.

She didn't know what love was. She knew all about betrayal and deception and greed, but nothing about love. Jackson saw the flashing red light on his phone, indicating the voice mail left by Laurie, and quickly hit Delete without bothering to listen to it. He didn't have time for such nonsense. She was obsessed with his money, nothing more.

He finished the first offer letter to Kent for the 1209 property and sent it off, pretty certain that it would be flat-out rejected. It was below market value of the building, but Jackson had to start somewhere. He figured they'd eventually meet in the middle if Kent really was serious about selling to him and this wasn't just some elaborate game. It could be. Kent no doubt would love the idea of just toying with Jackson, making him believe he had a chance at a property that Kent had no intention of selling. Kent didn't care so much about wasting their time as he did about annoying Jackson. Honestly, the man should get a hobby. Or a wife to keep him busy. Something.

Still, he liked the idea of being Chloe's landlord. He knew he could take better care of her and her building than Kent ever would. He liked the thought of dropping in, asking her if anything in her apartment needed fixing. There were certain things he'd like to fix right now, like the fact that he wanted to see her naked. In his bed.

This made him wonder if she'd responded to his question yet. He glanced at his calendar, which was thin for the rest of the afternoon. Maybe he'd just pop home and see.

He walked out of his office and saw Hailey typing at her desk. Then he remembered Chloe's smashed phone and the devastated look on her face when he'd returned her mangled device.

"Oh, Hailey, do we have any extra smartphones? I need a backup," he said.

Hailey didn't miss a beat as she turned to fetch a key from her drawer to unlock a cabinet near her knees. She pulled out a box and handed it to him.

"And a manila envelope, please?"

She handed it to him, no questions asked.

"Thanks, Hailey. I'll be back in an hour or so. Let me know if anything urgent comes in."

"Will do, sir," she said, and nodded at him, and then turned her attention back to her computer.

Jackson tucked the new phone into the envelope, and thought Chloe would be surprised when he showed up with a replacement for her smashed one. He remembered how absolutely brokenhearted she looked when she saw her phone fall from her window. She wouldn't have been sitting there if they hadn't been moving in, and so he figured the least he could do was replace it.

He liked the idea of getting her a gift, and whistled to himself as he took the elevator down to the parking garage. A quick drive home in his Maserati meant that he was pulling into the parking space near his condo a few minutes later. He glanced up, clearly seeing her message to him. It was spelled out in Post-it notes on her window.

Maybe.

He grinned. *Maybe* she wanted to do more than watch? Well, he'd have to get to work on convincing her he was worth the trouble. He carried the envelope holding the brand-new phone he'd taken from his office as a replacement for her cracked one. He scribbled a quick note there on the porch and slipped the piece of paper into the manila envelope. He took the package and laid it on top of her mailboxes and then rang her buzzer.

Chloe heard the buzzer, but finished the posts she was doing for her client on Instagram. She figured it was just another package delivery, though she couldn't remember what she'd ordered exactly. She finished up the post and then headed downstairs, swinging open her building's front door. A manila envelope sat on her mailboxes, addressed to her. Except it had no postage. Or mailing label. Just her name in thick black marker: Chloe Park. There was a small note inside. It read:

> *Chloe,*
> *"Maybe" sounds like you need more convincing that it's more fun to do than to watch. Call me if you need the reasons why.*
> *Jackson.*

Bewildered, she ripped open the package and found a *brand-new smartphone*. What the…? Her new, rich, tattoo-clad neighbor had just handed her an eight-hundred-dollar phone. She glanced at the mobile, shocked. Who did that? *Someone who owns a Maserati and a whole building.*

She fetched her cracked phone from her kitchen table, and then compared it to the sleek new phone. She couldn't believe this. Was he…for real? He didn't even know her. She couldn't accept a gift like this. Besides, what would his leggy, model girlfriend think? The one who showed up at his house not wearing a bra or underwear beneath that microjumper?

She glanced up at his building across the alleyway, but she couldn't see into his window from this angle, though she saw the blinds were open and it seemed like there might be a light on, but the daylight made it hard to tell. Should she march over there and give this back to him?

Or would he get the wrong idea and think she was there to do *more* than watch? But maybe that was exactly what she wanted to do.

She studied the phone. She couldn't keep it. It was too big a gift from someone she didn't even know.

You know what he looks like naked and you know how he can satisfy a woman. And not only is he up for a booty call, but he gave you the phone to do it.

Still, she told herself, tamping down her naughty thoughts. What if she took the phone and then he expected her to…*do* things in return?

Then again, that didn't sound bad. Not bad at all.

No. She had to give the phone back. She couldn't keep such an expensive gift. Right? It was crazy, wasn't it? Just as she debated what to do next, the new phone in her hand came to life with a standard ringtone.

What the…?

She glanced down at the phone and realized the thing was on. On and clearly activated, because a call was coming in from *Jackson Drake.*

Uh…should she answer? Should she ignore it? Why did the man give her a phone with his *number* programmed into it? No better time than now to tell him she couldn't accept such a gift.

"Hello?" she said as she pressed the phone to her ear.

"Hey, neighbor." Jackson's voice was like melted chocolate. Smooth, sexy, sweet.

"Oh…uh. Hi." When she looked at her windows, she saw the back of her own blinds. She'd drawn them after the show the night before, not trusting herself not to glance out once more. Her window was still open, though, since she didn't want to call the AC repair person just yet—not until a few more freelance checks came in. The light in her studio apartment was dim, so she flicked on the kitchen light and went to retrieve some water from the tap.

"I see you got my gift." His voice, warm, deep, made her own insides go gooey.

"Uh, right…about that… I mean, thank you so much. It's so generous of you, but…I don't think I can *accept* it."

"You don't like it?" Now Jackson sounded concerned. She almost felt he might run out and buy her a different one if she'd asked.

"No. No! I love it. I mean it's an amazing phone." And it was. The sound quality was so good, and the thing was so light, the screen so big, she knew from the commercials she'd seen that this was the brand-new, just out, must-have model.

"If you love it, then keep it."

"It's so expensive, and…I mean…"

"Chloe." He said her name as if he owned it. The determination in his voice sparked something inside her. Want? Or maybe more primal. Need. His voice rumbled through her chest and settled in her belly. "I have many phones for the Realtors at my office, and so, seriously, I insist. Take one. Otherwise, it'll just sit in a drawer and not get used."

"Well, if it's really no trouble, but I'll need to switch it to my plan and…"

"If you'd like," he said. "But even if you don't, that's fine as well. I'd insist you keep it. My gift to you. If the movers hadn't been such a distraction, you would've never dropped that phone."

The movers weren't the distraction, she thought. *You were.*

"Well, thank you. I mean it. The phone is…well, amazing. Thank you. I'd been worried about how to get a new one." Suddenly, she felt the weight of the gesture. It was nice of him, even if it wasn't any trouble for a man as wealthy as he was, and who else did she know who would give a brand-new phone to a perfect stranger?

"Well, then. Worry no more." The way he said it made her laugh a little.

"So, how did you know I'd gotten the phone? Have you been calling it?"

"No. I saw you pick it up."

Now she felt self-conscious, her face flushing hot. He was watching her door? That meant...

"Wait...you're home?"

"Why don't you open your blinds and see?"

Chloe's heart sped up, thumping like a caffeinated rabbit in her chest. He'd seen her? She leaped to the blinds and tugged on the string, even as she remembered that she hadn't had time to put on makeup since her shower. Still, she yanked up her blinds and there, across the alley, was Jackson, clad in a white undershirt that left nothing to the imagination, and shorts.

He grinned, a bright, shining smile, beneath that full, bad-boy goatee. He waved. Her heart leaped a little. God, the man was gorgeous. If he was a son of anarchy, then let the chaos begin.

"Hi," she said, and waved back, her voice catching in her throat. Then she felt silly. He was all the way across the alley, but even from this distance, she could feel the attraction. His blue eyes studied her even from behind his window.

"Hi, back," he said, in a tone that Chloe felt in the balls of her feet. The man's voice was so deep, so confident.

He grinned once more. She felt like an idiot, suddenly at a loss of what to say.

"Now my view just got a whole helluva lot better. Anyone ever tell you how gorgeous you are?"

"Me?" squeaked Chloe. She fanned her face, the

air in the apartment close and thick suddenly. Sweat broke out on her lower back. The wind had all but died. She felt the benefits of her earlier shower evaporate in the warm air. "But, I'm sweaty and…"

"I like sweaty." Oh, she knew he did. She remembered just how he liked to work up a sweat after watching him the night before. Chloe felt her face flush hot, and it had nothing to do with the warm summer air.

"I know you do. You got quite a workout last night." The words were out of her mouth before she even realized what she was saying. What on earth? Had she just brought up her peeping? There was something about that man's dangerous smile, the daring look on his face right now. She wanted to shock him.

Jackson chuckled. "Did you like what you saw?"

Chloe bit her lip. If she admitted she did, she was probably a pervert, but if she said no, she'd be lying. So she just stared at him, hand on the window. She gave a slow nod. "That was…*quite* a performance."

Jackson laughed again, a deep rumble that she felt in the back of her knees.

"Good," he said, his eyes never leaving hers.

"I—I never do that. I usually…"

"Close the blinds before you get to the good stuff?" Jackson slowly shook his head and wagged a disapproving finger. "Why would you do that?"

Now Chloe did laugh, nervously. Why did he make her feel like it was totally okay to watch him? Why wasn't he more upset? The whole thing was just…

crazy, but the way Jackson was looking at her right at that moment, through the window, made her think it was all somehow normal. No, not just normal… right. Was it right?

She remembered how turned on she'd been watching him. Wasn't that…wrong? I mean, how could she *like* watching him and his girlfriend? Also, what if she'd noticed her—the uninvited guest?

"Well…I shouldn't have. I promise next time, I'll let you have your privacy."

Jackson cocked his head to one side. "What if I don't want my privacy?" This sent a tingle down the back of her legs. "What if I *like* you watching?"

Now Chloe was speechless. He *had* liked it. She knew on some level this was true, but now he'd admitted it. Her lips parted, and she realized she had no idea what to say.

"What if I want you to watch?" He moved closer to the window, pressing his palm against it, as he glanced up at her. "What if I want you to do *more* than watch?"

Her throat went dry and she swallowed—hard.

"Well, I'm sure your girlfriend might feel differently." There. She'd said it!

Jackson frowned and gave a single shoulder shrug. "Oh, she's not my girlfriend."

Suddenly, Chloe felt a hard pit in her stomach. Not his girlfriend? Oh, please not something more… She hoped not fiancée or…even worse, his wife!

"What is she?"

"Just a friend." Jackson's tone was all business.

She remembered the night before, how he'd been so deep inside her, thrusting again and again, each time ever deeper. Longer. Harder. "You didn't *look* like just friends."

"We sometimes take advantage of certain benefits," he added.

"Friends with benefits."

"Actually, to be honest, more like just the benefits. Annaliese…prefers it that way. We rarely talk, except…well, about positions." He chuckled a little. "And speed."

Chloe swallowed the excitement building in her. The woman didn't mean anything to him, not in any real way. She remembered how his eyes lit up when he saw her watching. Did that mean she excited him even more than Annaliese?

"Chloe, I was wondering…"

Was he going to invite her over? The thought sent a shiver of excitement down the back of her legs.

"Aren't you hot? I'm feeling a little bit warm." Jackson pulled at the hem of his shirt and then whipped it over his head. Chloe sucked in a breath. The man was all brawn and tattoos, a dangerous combination that immediately sent her heart racing. Her attention lingered on the glorious vee that dipped into the waistband of his shorts. He glanced up at her, expression playful. "Now, your turn."

"Mine?" Oh, God. Was she going to take off her shirt? Was she seriously going to do this?

"Only if you want to." He grinned. Part of her did want to—that was the crazy thing!

Then she remembered that beneath her tank was one of her newest sports bras. It had a sexy vee, a keyhole and lots of crisscrossing straps. At least she'd had the foresight to wear one today. It had full coverage and was hardly scandalous, but it did lift the girls, a hint of cleavage at the neckline. She could remove her shirt and be wearing more than she did on the beach.

"I don't want you to do anything you're not comfortable doing. And, besides, I'm over here. I can't even touch you."

That's the only problem, she thought.

"Fine." She tugged off her tank, revealing the low-cut push-up bra.

"You're beautiful," he said, awe in his voice. "I want to see more."

"You first."

He grinned, just the hint of a smile on his face. He didn't hesitate as he put his thumbs into the waistband of his shorts and tugged them down. In seconds, she saw his dark blue boxer briefs that left absolutely nothing to the imagination, the bulge in the front of them enormous. She hadn't imagined the size of him the night before. Even not standing at attention, his bulge was impressive. Everywhere she looked she saw tight, taut muscle, a man built for sex.

"Your turn." He cocked his head to one side, anticipating her next move.

Well, I'm in this far, she thought. She cautiously

slipped out of her yoga capris, revealing a low-cut black string bikini. She inwardly felt grateful she wasn't wearing an embarrassing print one—with red cherries or the ones covered in a Wonder Woman emblem.

"You're gorgeous," Jackson breathed, a murmur in her ear, as he looked at her appreciatively. "I wish I could touch you."

"Me, too," she barely whispered, not believing she could actually be this bold. Was it the alleyway that separated them? The glass? She felt like a different person somehow, and yet…very much herself at the same time.

"If I stare at you much longer, I'm going to need to take these off." His hands skimmed the front of his underwear.

Her heart thudded like a bass drum beating in her chest. Yes. That's what she wanted. To see him naked again. To see his powerful self, fully and completely on display for her. She wanted to see all of him. And, she realized with a shock, she wanted him to see her, too.

Then she heard a high-pitched whistle. "Nice undies!" shouted a garbageman from the alleyway. She'd been so engrossed in Jackson, she'd missed the city worker who was wheeling trash cans to his truck waiting near the curb by the sidewalk. Instinctively, she covered herself with one arm and backed away from the window, her face feeling like it was on fire. She wrapped the curtain around herself, toga-style.

"I'm going to demolish that jerk," Jackson said,

pecs flexing as he glared down at the garbageman. He was all mean brawn, and for a second, Chloe imagined he would literally destroy the out-of-shape city worker if given the chance.

"No, it's okay. I'm standing half-naked in front of my window!"

"I'm sorry about that," Jackson said, frowning. "I'll go down there and make sure he doesn't look in your window ever again."

Chloe had visions of the city worker beaten to a pulp.

"No! That's okay. I'm fine. Really."

"You sure?"

"Yeah." Chloe grinned, still feeling self-conscious, her heart beating wildly. What did she expect? She was half-naked during the day in front of her own window!

"I feel responsible." Jackson looked contrite. "Let me make it up to you."

"How?"

"Let me take you out to dinner."

CHAPTER FIVE

CHLOE SPENT THE rest of the afternoon trying to figure out what to wear, even though part of her hoped that at the end of the night, she'd leave all her clothes on Jackson's floor. She imagined a dozen scenarios, all of which ended with him taking her on his couch, in full view of that window, just like he had Annaliese. Her stomach twisted into a knot when she thought of the gorgeous model-thin waif he'd had. It shouldn't turn her on so much and yet every time she thought about it, she felt a little tickle in her tummy. Friends with benefits, he'd said. Or, really, just benefits. But how many of those did he have? And was she going to fill yet another spot in his schedule?

She wondered.

She also wondered if she really cared.

It had been months since Kevin called her the wrong name in bed. Months since she'd broken it off with the man who failed to truly see her. Who didn't understand what she did for a living or why she did it, who forgot her very name in the most intimate of moments. She was ready to move on, she decided. She'd hidden in her apartment long enough.

Her buzzer rang promptly at seven, and Chloe gave a hasty check of her appearance in the mirror: short sundress, strappy, sexy heels, her hair up in a messy, thrown-together way that took her nearly an hour to perfect. Her stomach buzzed with nerves as she grabbed her small cross-body bag and headed for the door. The last thing she saw before she'd headed to the hallway was Jackson's darkened window, and with a thrill, she realized she might be there later that very night.

When she swung open her glass front door, Jackson stood on the stoop, dressed in a starched collared shirt, open to the third button, and jeans, looking every inch the billionaire…and the bad boy, a hint of his tattoo visible near the open collar of his shirt. His stark blue eyes lit up when he saw her as he gave a low, almost wolfish whistle.

"You're a knockout," he said, and she felt a blush creep up her neck.

"So are you… I mean, even with clothes on." She laughed an anxious laugh and he joined her. It was strange. She'd seen him completely naked, and yet with clothes, he seemed even sexier somehow.

"Did I mention you're gorgeous?" He leaned in to give her a hug. He pressed her to his chest, and she felt herself melt into him. "I'll be staring at you all night," he whispered in her ear, and she felt his hot breath on her neck.

"I hope so," she blurted, before she knew she was speaking her thoughts aloud, and the blush grew hotter. "I mean, good."

He pulled away and grinned. His blue eyes sparkled. "You sure you want to go to dinner?" He nodded up at his apartment. "We could order in."

Yes. That's a fantastic idea, she was about to say before she caught herself. What was it about him that made her throw caution to the wind—and her clothes as well, if earlier was any indication? Then her stomach grumbled—loudly.

He frowned, ever so slightly. "Nope, better get some food in you," he said. "Our car awaits."

"Car?" she asked, thinking of the Maserati she saw the first day, but then he nodded to the sleek Bentley waiting at the curb. A driver in a jacket and dark pants waited for them, holding open the back door.

Chloe felt her mouth drop open. She'd never ridden in a limo before. In a *Bentley* limo. No wonder he had gorgeous women at his beck and call. Who wouldn't want this kind of luxury?

"I find it's easier this way. So I can drink and not worry." He took her arm and led her to the car. She ducked into the plush leather seats that smelled new, and waited for him to walk around the car and join her in the back seat. He slid in next to her, and Chloe felt his body heat as his leg pressed into hers. She glanced around the car feeling a little bit uneasy.

How could a man who had all of this ever settle for just one woman?

And why am I thinking about that, anyway? I'm supposed to be looking for a rebound, like Ryan suggested. Why am I even thinking this isn't going to be anything but amazing sex? Superhot, naughty sex?

"Where are we going?" she asked him.

"That depends. Do you feel like champagne and caviar or whiskey and pork belly?"

Chloe didn't hesitate. "I love whiskey, so that's my vote."

She'd had her share of craft whiskeys and bourbons, something her light beer–drinking ex never quite understood. But Chloe liked what she liked, and she wasn't going to make apologies for it.

Surprise flickered across Jackson's features as he studied her in the darkened back seat of the Bentley. Chicago slid by them, the city beginning to come to life as the summer sun hit the horizon.

"A girl who loves whiskey? You're after my own heart."

Chloe felt a little glow of warmth in her chest.

"I've never been a frilly, white-wine-with-an-ice-cube kind of girl."

He laughed a little. "Then you're my kind of girl." Jackson held her gaze for a beat, his blue eyes promising more.

"Ed," Jackson said, addressing his driver, but

never moving his gaze from her face. "Take us to Longman in Logan Square."

The sun had just set as they zoomed west, away from sparkling Lake Michigan, and down Diversey, the streetlights flickering on as they drove past boutiques and little cafés on their way to Logan Square, one of Chicago's eclectic, diverse neighborhoods west of downtown, known for attracting aspiring artists and musicians.

Chloe could feel Jackson's attention on her as they drove through the darkening summer dusk.

"What are you thinking about?" he asked her.

About you, naked, taking me every which way possible.

"Uh…what do you do for a living? To afford a Bentley?"

"Real estate." Jackson shrugged. "I used to be a bartender, actually, but then my dad died of a heart attack and left me insurance money. I bought up some bankrupt properties at the right time, fixed them up myself and made quite a profit. Now I've got a little company."

The Bentley rolled past a billboard-sized ad painted across a nearby building that read *Drake Properties*.

"Wait—that's you? Drake Properties? I see those signs everywhere."

"I get around." He grinned as he stroked his goatee. She wanted to do the same.

"Must be weird." She couldn't even begin to imagine what it would be like to be a real estate magnate. They drove past a bar advertising Chicago's local Goose Island brew as throngs of people crowded the sidewalks.

"Why?" He seemed puzzled.

"Because you go from just ordinary bartender to über-rich guy in a short amount of time. What's the best thing about being rich?"

Jackson glanced out the window. She got the impression that he didn't like to talk about money. "I dunno. Not worrying, I guess."

"And the worst?"

His attention snapped back to her, sharp blue eyes intelligent and calculating. "You think there's something bad about being rich?"

"I'm sure there is. What do they say…mo' money, mo' problems?"

He focused on her intently. She felt the weight of his gaze.

"Nobody has ever asked me that before."

Chloe grinned. "Well, I guess I'm not like anybody else you've met."

Jackson's eyes sparkled. "No, you're not."

"So what is the worst thing about being rich?"

"Being invisible," Jackson answered quickly, without hesitation.

She glanced around the inside of their slick limo.

"That can't be," she said. "I mean, you've got this flashy car, and tons of cash, and isn't that the opposite of being invisible?"

Jackson shrugged. "People start to see just the money. They don't care about the monkey in the monkey suit anymore, it's just the label on the suit that matters. My last girlfriend only saw me as walking dollar signs. She tried to get pregnant—on purpose behind my back. She used one of our... condoms, if you can believe it. To try to get child support."

"That's awful!" How could a woman do that? Chloe couldn't imagine the cold calculations that would lead a woman to do something like that. Chloe would only ever want to have a baby for love, with a partner she'd trust to be a good father. Having one simply to get money was something that had never occurred to her.

"Well, it happens, more often than you'd think. People don't see me. They just see what I can buy." He shrugged a beefy shoulder, as if he'd long ago become resigned to this fact.

"I know what it's like to be invisible," Chloe said, thinking that she had more in common with her hunky neighbor than just attraction. "My old boyfriend never saw me. He even called me by another woman's name. During...you know..."

"What?" Jackson sat straight up, his spine rigid. "How could he do that?"

"He just never really saw me. I just fit a role in his life, but he never really cared about me."

"He's an idiot. And he's blind. You're gorgeous."

Chloe felt her insides grow warm at the compliment. Jackson reached over and took her hand, and she felt a little electric current run up her arm. His hand was so big and warm.

They arrived at the famous whiskey bar in Logan Square and Jackson breezed in, and after a few words to the hostess, managed to snag them a corner table in the crowded restaurant with the masculine decor, the wooden ceilings, the long dark bar, and the wood-and-metal bar stools that gave the bar an antique and rustic feel at the same time. The menu was anything but rustic, however, as Chloe saw foie gras among many of the small-plate offerings.

"How did we get a table so fast?" she asked him, noticing the crowd of patrons waiting for seats at the bar.

"They know me," he said and shrugged.

Chloe let that sink in for a minute. She wondered how many other connections he had around the city. She could see why women would be impressed, dazzled by the man's money and his influence, but what about the man?

"So, a man like you, who seems to have everything." She glanced out the front window at the Bentley that slid away from the curb outside, the driver who would be back for them later. "You've got all your needs taken care of. So what is it that you still want?"

He hesitated, mulling over her question, as they both looked over the menu.

"Conversation, like we're having now," he said, and grinned at her.

"You can't be serious. You have...Annaliese. And..."

He laughed a little sheepishly. "I know it sounds crazy, but I want more than that. I always have. A family, a partner. Something long-term."

"You want to give up the literal wet dream of every man I know. All the sex he can handle, but none of the responsibility." Chloe rolled her eyes, and he laughed. She liked that he could take her ribbing, that he wasn't ultrasensitive. Guys with fragile egos were a major turnoff. Chloe thought about Kevin, about how he'd ultimately looked to other women to constantly validate himself. He didn't feel like a man unless he was cheating. It was sad, really.

The waiter materialized, and he ordered two of their finest whiskeys.

"I want a real relationship," he said. "I want a real connection. Someone special to share my success with, but I've almost given up on finding that person."

"Why? Because of your ex?"

He nodded, looking a bit sad.

"It's just...hard to be put in a box," he added now. "Women see the money and then, well, they don't care about anything else. I'd dismiss the friends with benefits in a heartbeat if I found the real partner."

"Really?"

"Really." Jackson fixed her with a serious stare.

His blue eyes flashed with honesty. A little bit of hope flared in her chest. Maybe he wasn't a hopeless playboy after all. Maybe she wasn't crazy in thinking the connection they had might go beyond the physical.

"So, am I here auditioning for the part of friend with benefits? Or…something else?"

A slow smile spread across his face. "Which will get you into my bed faster?"

Chloe threw back her head and laughed. She loved flirting with this man, loved the raw, powerful energy she felt coming off him in waves. She dared not answer that question, because she was pretty sure she'd slip into his bed without any trouble at all.

Jackson grinned as the waiter delivered their drinks and the two clinked glasses. Chloe sipped at the cool amber liquid, amazed at its taste. This was far beyond Jack Daniel's.

"So, time for me to ask you, a beautiful, single and successful woman like yourself… What do you want?"

"I'm not as successful as you," she conceded as she took a sip of her rich aged rye whiskey.

"You are renting an expensive apartment without a roommate. You work from home, and you've got your own little social media empire there and you're younger than thirty. I'd say you're pretty successful."

Chloe put down the glass. The candle at the center of their table flickered in the dim light of the bar, as shadows danced across Jackson's handsome face.

"That's true," Chloe said, but failed to add that sometimes paying bills was tight. She supposed she did all right in the balance. When her tax refund came in, then she paid down debt and even had extra to tuck away in an IRA. Still, she'd be lying if she said she didn't envy Jackson's independent wealth. Who wouldn't want to not worry about where the next car payment was coming from?

They shared a batch of delicious small plates and another round of drinks, and Chloe found her head spinning from the rich food, the good company and the amber whiskey in her glass. She found herself jumping ahead, wondering what it would be like to date someone like Jackson Drake. Or was this just how he treated all his "friends with benefits"?

She watched as the waitress kept her eyes on Jackson, the way she took note of his Rolex watch.

"Why did you convert the building next door?" she asked him. "Why did you want all that space?"

Jackson shrugged. "I guess I wanted to be in the city, but I didn't want neighbors."

Chloe cocked an eyebrow. "You've got me."

"You're a beautiful neighbor," he said, correcting himself. "I was more worried about disturbing them, actually, with some of the noise I make."

"Having sex with beautiful girls?" Chloe quirked an eyebrow as she took a sip of her drink.

Jackson let out a bark of a laugh. "Well, yes and no. I have a workshop. For woodwork. I like to work with my hands, always have," he explained. "Since

I started my company, I do less of that, but I'd like to do more."

Chloe felt a ripple of surprise. The man made things? Next, he'd tell her he was into other manly things: riding motorcycles, hunting, chopping down trees. She wouldn't be surprised. It would explain his bulging muscles.

"What do you make?"

"Furniture, mostly. Antique bar stools. Tables. That sort of thing." Jackson nodded toward the bar with the old swivel bar stools: wooden on top, antique metal on the bottom. "I made those."

"You *made* those?" Chloe gaped at the stools lining the dark oak bar.

"I found the metal, those old pipes, in a building I bought in Printer's Row, an old pipe manufacturer that Al Capone once used to store some of his bootleg. The city is full of amazing antiques, some right in front of you, and with a little elbow grease, you can reuse them, repurpose them."

"I love that. It's one of the things I love about Chicago, about how it's both an old city and a new one, all at once." Chloe felt like in that moment they shared a brain. Her friends never quite understood her fascination with both old and new.

"It's what I love about the city, too," he said. "It's why I like to take old buildings and make them livable and usable again.

"It's a hobby." Jackson took a drink. "When I was first flipping properties, I'd go to stage them with furniture, but never really liked what I found. Sometimes, I'd end up making my own pieces. It's what my dad did for a living, actually. I'd probably be a carpenter like him if I hadn't made those real estate investments."

"Which do you like doing more?"

"I like them both," he admitted. "The woodworking gives me something to do with my hands."

Chloe remembered just how well he'd used his hands.

"I'd like to see your shop sometime."

"Really?"

"Yeah, I would. I admire that you make things. All of my work is in the virtual world, so sometimes I feel like I've got nothing to show for all the hours I've put in." Chloe shrugged.

"But today, social media is everything," Jackson said. "Maybe you could help with Drake Properties, too. If you're taking new clients."

Would she! "Uh, yeah, I—I'd love to work with you. I mean, what an honor! You'd be more than welcome as a client." Chloe failed to mention he'd automatically be her biggest client. The second being a well-known consulting firm in town. But she had no client as high-profile as Drake Properties.

"Right now, we don't have a centralized media presence. I have an assistant who posts to my account and then, of course, we have individual agents." Jackson pulled up an account and showed her the feed.

Chloe thumbed through the feed and nodded.

"This is typical of businesses with a lot of independent contractors," she said. "You've got a lot of individual posts, agents selling or flipping properties, but you don't have a cohesive social media message from the corporation itself. We can change that."

"Can you?" Jackson looked at Chloe appreciatively. She felt a little blush creep up her cheeks.

"Yes, and you can leverage the followers your individual agents already have. I can work out a plan for you. We can make this happen." Chloe felt confident she could get a lot of buzz going about Drake Properties, especially since it was already practically a household name in Chicago. Social media was all about understanding how to tap into the power of people.

"You seem to be a woman of many talents." He studied her over his now-empty plate and Chloe felt rooted to the spot. She'd never felt so *visible* before, so fully and openly seen. There was something about the way Jackson studied her, the way he asked her questions, the way he listened, that made her feel he was fully present. She hadn't felt this valued since the last time she'd had dinner with her parents, who lived in Seattle and came to Chicago twice a year. It was always an interrogation fest, as her mom worked to make up for lost time. Chloe was their only child, but they also just retired and spent a fair amount of their time traveling.

She liked being the focus of Jackson's attention. She felt like she knew him, almost as if she'd known him much longer than just a couple of days. *Then again, I did see him...naked. And...intimate. Why wouldn't I feel intimacy?*

Chloe knew she was getting ahead of herself— again. She was a planner and liked to think three or four moves ahead, and she hadn't even slept with Jackson yet and she was already trying to figure out if they *worked*. Why couldn't she just turn her brain off and...enjoy this? Why did she have to analyze every angle?

It was what made her a good social media publicist, though, thinking through scenarios, predicting outcomes.

Chloe felt full, her head spinning with whiskey and with the proximity to Jackson's fit body. The longer the dinner wore on, the more Chloe was aware what might be coming after. She'd been keenly aware of the skin she could see: his strong forearms, his strong, thick neck, braided with muscle; and more than aware of the skin hidden beneath his clothes, and the very impressive bits of him that lay covered still. She was both eager and anxious all at the same time to see them once more.

What if he was actually too big for her? Then again, what if he were the very best sex of her life? Throughout dinner, she felt like she was walking a knife's blade of anticipation. It hadn't even occurred to her *not* to sleep with him.

The waiter set the bill on the table and they both reached for it.

"No," Jackson said, shaking his head firmly. "I said I'd buy."

"But can I help?" She didn't want him to think she was one of those girls who was just after his money. And she did make her own. She could help pay her own way.

"Not this time," he said. "My treat."

Reluctantly, she let him take the check. He paid for it with a luxury credit card, one of those heavy metal cards that could probably take a bullet in an emergency. It hit the table with a *thunk* and she eyed it, wondering if this was just one more way the rich were different. They carried around cards made of *literal* platinum.

"Are you in the mood for dessert?" he asked her.

"Are you?" she asked, uncertain about what he had in mind.

"I am interested in dessert." He studied her, amusement in his eyes. "But only the kind we have at my place."

CHAPTER SIX

JACKSON FELT AN impatience welling in him as they left the restaurant and ducked into the back seat of his Bentley. He'd known from the second he saw Chloe watching him from her fourth-floor window that he wanted her, and having dinner together only increased his desire. Throughout dinner, he'd been mesmerized by her dark, knowing eyes, the same eyes that had watched him the night before when he'd been with Annaliese, those eyes that had driven him to heights he hadn't felt in years. She'd even offered to pay some of the bill.

Only after you'd admitted most women only want you for your money, a nagging little cynical voice in his head said. *She could still be playing you.*

Yet something told him she wasn't. She'd been genuinely interested in the furniture he made, which astounded him. Most women found it boring, because that was a hobby that didn't make him much money. For the time he put into each piece, they cost more to make than to sell, but he still enjoyed the work, and the feeling of making something useful. And he loved *talking* with her, loved the way her mind worked, loved her quirky sense of humor. It was the first time in a long time he'd found a woman's brain as sexy as her body, and he wondered if that played a part in fueling his desire.

He wasn't going to get ahead of himself. Not this time. If he really analyzed his feelings, which he had no intention of doing, he'd probably figure out that rushing into sex was his way of avoiding feeling at all. Desire and want—well, those things were easily solved. Love and intimacy? Those were complicated animals, best left alone, since pursuing them inevitably led to disappointment.

He held her hand as his driver, Ed, thumped the door shut and slipped behind the wheel. There was no partition between the back seat and the front, but Ed normally kept to himself, a man of few words but excellent driving skills, and was an ex-Beret. Jackson kept him purely on a part-time basis, but Ed was happy to be his exclusive driver, especially since he got to drive the Bentley.

"Home, please, Ed," he told him, and he nodded, pulling away from the curb without another word. Chloe had grown quiet in the car, her face obscured by shadows, and the streetlights occasionally illuminating her big, dark eyes. He ran his finger up the soft skin of her bare arm, and she shivered beneath this touch. How he wanted her to watch him do all kinds of unspeakable things to her. Her lips parted, ever so slightly, as if she were about to say some-

thing, but then caught herself. He saw the outline of
her full lips in the streetlights flickering by. How he
wanted to taste them.

He glanced at Ed, in the front seat, his eyes fixed
on the road. No, he wouldn't kiss her. Not yet. He
moved his hand downward, toward the hem of her
skirt, which hit just above the knee. He traced the
amazing caramel-colored skin there with one finger, silently asking a question. When she glanced at
him, dark eyes welcoming the touch, he continued
his exploration. Ever so slightly, she shifted, moving
her knees a little apart: an invitation.

She glanced down, watching his hands as they
moved up to her inner thigh. He gave just a little
squeeze there, and she sucked in a breath. God, her
skin was so soft. His hand disappeared beneath the
fabric of her short sundress and went farther up her
leg. He saw her glance up at Ed, his back to them, his
eyes fixed on the road. Her lips were slightly parted,
pupils dark and wide. He stroked her inner thigh and
felt the goose bumps rise there as he moved ever upward. She spread her knees even wider apart, an invitation. He gently, so softly, felt the edge of her lacy
thong. He stroked her through the fine fabric and he
could feel her heat, her want, there.

Her eyes flickered closed as she leaned backward
into the leather seat, her chest rising. He could see
her nipples rise against the thin lace of her halter
bra, her back arching while her full breasts struggled
against the thin fabric of her sundress. He teased

her, rubbing her lightly and then softly, a caress that promised more to come. She welcomed him there, her legs stretching apart even more as he stoked the flame of her heat. Her breath deepened and a flush crept up the side of her face. She was primed for him. He could feel just how ready she was, her desire soaking the thin lace lining of her underwear. Unable to help himself, his finger slipped past the thin barrier and then he felt her bare: hot, willing and wet. God, she was so wet, so slick beneath his fingers. He wanted her. Wanted her now.

His own groin grew tight then, straining against the confines of his pants. Then, amazingly, she reached out for him, her hand covering the growing bulge, working her fingers across him, making him stiffen even more. Soon, he'd have to unzip himself just to relieve the pressure. She looked at him now, her dark eyes full of mischief and daring as they shared this dirty secret, Ed none the wiser as he slowed at a stoplight on Fullerton.

Now, with her hand on him, he couldn't wait. He pulled her to him with his free hand and kissed her, pressing his lips against hers, wanting to devour her. The kiss turned white-hot as he continued to explore her with his fingers. She opened her mouth to him and he tasted her with his tongue, his goatee brushing against her chin. Below, he felt her clench tightly around his fingers. God, so tight. How he wanted to explore the deepest, warmest part of her. She kept her hand on him as well, and he pressed against her hand, desperate for more of her touch. He strained against the confines of his pants.

Ed might have seen them by now, his green eyes in the rearview mirror, but Jackson didn't care. He was paid well for his discretion. Chloe didn't seem to care they had an audience, either. Did she like to be watched, almost as much as she liked to watch? The naughty thought thrilled him. Yes, this is what he wanted, a woman who was daring, who was bold, who knew what she wanted and went for it. That was what had turned him on so much when she'd watched him through his window. This was a woman who wasn't afraid.

He deepened the kiss and their tongues met in a kind of heated, primal dance. Instinct took over as he pushed his finger deeper inside her, finding the delicious ridges that he knew would be her most sensitive spot. She groaned into his mouth. He felt her delicious warm wetness. He wanted her. He wanted her now. Then, the car came to a stop and Ed cleared his throat, loudly, before opening and shutting his door—a cue to him as he realized with a start they now sat in the alley near his building. Had they kissed the entire way home? Her delicious scent still clung to his fingers when he pulled away from her and she tugged down the hem of her skirt.

Ed opened the door and Chloe got out, face flushed. Jackson watched her toned, tanned legs as they moved from the car before he followed her out.

"Thanks, Ed. That'll be all tonight."

Ed just gave a curt nod and ducked into the driver's seat without a word. Once he backed away from the door, Jackson slipped his hand around Chloe's lower back and pushed a code into his back door keypad. The door swung open.

They kissed again once inside the door, passionate, urgent, the door still half-open, as he pressed her to the wall, his hand running up the outside of her leg. His tongue dived deeper into her mouth. She tasted so good, all he wanted to do was kiss her again and again. Finally, he broke away, panting. He saw her in the dim light of his staircase, lips swollen from kissing, dark hair ruffled and eyes fixed on him.

"Let's go upstairs," she suggested. Before he could argue she was tugging him by the hand, up the two flights of dimly lit stairs to his living room. He strained against his pants the entire way, finding walking awkward since he wanted her so badly. He would've done her in the stairwell, hot, urgent, eager. But he soon realized she wanted to be in the room before his open windows. She flicked on the lamp, the same light he'd had on the night before. She walked to the window and glanced out, up at her own apartment, just across the alley. Her apartment was dark now, the alley deserted.

When she turned to face him, she slipped one spaghetti strap of her sundress down her shoulder. Then came the other one, and before he knew it, she'd shimmied out of it, letting it fall to the ground in a soft heap of cotton.

She stood before him in a lace halter bra and matching thong, her breasts large and heavy, yet seeming to defy gravity. Then she walked to him, all gorgeous curves. He wanted to memorize every one of those delicious lines and taste every inch of that soft skin. He bent down to kiss her, and he reached around her back, undoing the halter bra fastener with one hand, releasing her full breasts. He cupped them, and she moaned, arching her back, filling his hands. Then she found the hem of his shirt. She tugged it up, and then he was out of it. She pulled away, tracing her pink nails down the front of his bare skin. He shivered at her touch, straining against the strict confines of his pants. He needed to be free, and she sensed that as she found the zipper of his pants. She released him, and he stepped out of his pants and boxer briefs, standing bare before her. She dived in, working him hard with both her hands. Now it was his turn to groan.

"You're even bigger than I thought, and I thought you were big," she murmured into his mouth.

"It's all for you," he said, and meant it. He wanted every inch of himself inside her. Her hands worked the length of him as his need grew. She pulled back and their eyes met, an electric current zapping between them. Her dark gaze drove him wild. Even as she stared at him now, topless, her nipples puckering, he grew harder in her hands. This is what he wanted: her eyes watching him. Watching every move he made.

She released him and then tugged down her thong so it fell to the floor.

"Do me…like you did her," she commanded, voice low.

Yes, he thought, he would take her just like he'd had Annaliese the night before. Wrong on some level, maybe. Yet on another, ever so right. He flipped her over, kneading the firm skin of her rounded backside, now all of her inner pinkness in full view. He reached down and grabbed a Magnum condom from the pocket of his pants on the floor, anticipation running through him. The moment he'd been waiting for, he'd fantasized about, was here.

CHAPTER SEVEN

CHLOE WAITED, HER body an electric current of want as
she bent over the couch, Jackson behind her. Could
she take all of him? He was…so big. All of her lovers had been pretty much adequate to average, or
even the small side of average.

Chloe felt Jackson rub his thick tip against her
thighs. So big. So monstrously big.

She remembered Annaliese's face from the night
before, pure ecstasy as she took him. All of him.
Now it was her turn. But first, Jackson teased her.
He rubbed himself against her. She didn't think she
could be more turned on, and yet as he touched her,
she grew hotter, the need burning inside her like
a flame. She glanced out his windows and saw a
light come on in her building, a single yellow square
across the alley.

For a second, she worried her neighbor would
see her, just as she'd seen Annaliese and Jackson
the night before.

But then he slipped the massive knob of his tip inside her and all worry about modesty fled her mind.

He pushed in an inch, maybe more, parting her, testing her wetness. God, so big. So hard. Just the first part. He worked himself slowly, gently, teasing her, making her want even more. Now it was all she could do not to cry out. He wasn't even all the way in yet, and she was parted in a way she'd never been. *Yes*, she thought. *Yes. I want you. All you can give me.*

She glanced at another square of light across the alley beneath closed blinds. Did she care if she was seen? She didn't care. Let them watch.

This is what I needed. What I've always needed.

"Do you want more?" he asked her, voice a low rumble.

"Yes," she croaked, a slave to her own desire, her own need to have him. All of him. In full view of her neighbors. She didn't care. Couldn't care. All she thought about was him behind her as he pushed forward a little deeper. She cried out in pleasure as he stretched her even more. She was so full, so deliciously full.

"More?"

"More!" she cried out, wondering how much more she could take. Then again, she was so very wet, her body willing to take all of him. He slid in the full length of himself, and she nearly came right then as he pressed her limits, finding the deepest, virgin parts of her. Only he had been this deep. Only he had parted her like this.

"Oh, God…" he murmured, voice catching in his throat. "You're so…tight. So very tight."

She burned with need, with want, with over-whelming desire. Then he slid out, ever so slowly, before moving right back in. Chloe barely noticed the windows now, her thoughts focused on the sensations running through her body. Oh, God. She was going to come right now. She'd never felt like this before, never realized how primal sex could be. She was a slave to his power, to his pure physical domination as he took her, harder now, from behind, reaching deeper inside her, setting her on fire as he made her burn for him again and again. She was going to come, and she'd never come this way before, never come with a man taking her from behind. Yet now she knew exactly how Annaliese felt, bent over the couch, dominated by a man who was born to pleasure a woman. No wonder she'd come so quickly. How could she resist? How could she *not* come, not when every inch of her cried out to come, to shout for mercy? Watching him had been amazing, but nothing compared to being with him, to having him inside her, so very deep.

A light across the alley flickered off. Another, on the second floor, came on, and a man walked across it, yawning, not having seen them. If he looked up... he'd see everything. But he didn't, and instead, sauntered out of view.

So dangerous. So deliciously wrong. They should shut the blinds.

Yet part of Chloe liked being wild, liked feeling like a primal animal in a city where laws were supposed to rein in desire, pin people in. Yes, this was what she wanted. To be on display, just like Annaliese the night before, to let everybody see that Jackson desired her, wanted her, was so very hard for her. *He wants me*, the open windows shouted to the world. *He's having me. He's making me come.*

Jackson thrust harder and she vaulted over the edge, hitting a peak of pleasure she'd never felt before. She cried out his name then, hoarse, raw, as he gripped her hips hard, riding her as she came, pushing inside her, deeper, for every wave of pleasure, making every ripple of her climax last longer than she thought possible. Her whole body contracted and shuddered in wave after wave of pure pleasure she'd never felt before. As the last bit of her shocking climax ebbed away, he slowed, and she wondered how she could continue. Her knees had grown weak, her legs shaking from spent passion. He withdrew, and she collapsed atop his couch.

"I want to see you," he said, and turned her over. She saw him then, his impressive physical prowess, and still couldn't believe his size. She'd taken that. She'd taken it all. He moved her so that she was lying on her back on the couch and moved to take her once more. Could she do this? She felt so spent, so worn, and yet, as she gazed up at his sharp blue eyes, her body came alive again. Those eyes, she thought. Her heart pumped harder, just like it had when she'd met his gaze through the window. Could it be she wasn't yet satisfied? It was true. She wanted him once more.

He pushed into her again, stretching her to her limits.

She wondered if he could even move inside her, and yet somehow he did. He was above her now, his eyes watching her as she touched his chest, slipping down his shoulder tattoo now visible to her. It was the wing of a dragon. Big, strong, powerful.

"Chloe," he moaned. His breath came sharply. "I don't know if I can…if I can hold it." She could see the strain in his face. She felt his need for her as he picked up the pace, as he slid in and out, as he seemed to amazingly grow harder, bigger, inside her. Every nerve ending in her body came alive as she once again began a steady climb to another climax. She felt the need building in her, the red-hot desire. She saw a dim reflection of herself in his steely blue eyes, she saw how much he wanted her as well, and that knowledge drove her wild.

"I can't hold it. I can't…" He fought, but lost the battle, though it didn't matter, because after a few more deep thrusts, she once again found herself swept up in a tidal wave of uncontrollable pleasure. She shut her eyes against the rush of pure release, a shout ripped from her throat as she was powerless to stop it. He cried out, too, and then he collapsed on top of her, their sweat-slicked bodies sliding to-gether in delicious harmony. Chloe felt the weight of him on her, the delicious weight, her chest pressed against his taut muscles. The man was all muscle. All raw power.

"I'm sorry. I usually, uh, last longer than that." Jackson looked sheepish as he pulled himself up on his elbows.

"I came twice," Chloe breathed. "I think you lasted long enough."

He chuckled, a rumble she could feel with his belly pressed against hers, him slowly softening inside her.

"You were…" His blue eyes sparkled. "So deliciously tight. I couldn't help it. You made me come so fast."

A blush crept up her cheek. "I'd never had someone so big, uh, before."

"Good," he said, eyes never leaving her face. She glanced at the open windows.

"I've never—" She nodded to the open windows. "I mean—" She paused. "Do you always…"

"Leave the blinds open?" He grinned. "Sometimes. Sometimes not, but there's something about being on display that's hot. Don't you agree?"

Chloe nodded vigorously. "I just never thought I'd do something like this."

"I wonder what else we can try next time." He shot her a wolfish grin and Chloe felt anticipation tickle her toes. *Next time*—that implied there'd be one.

Jackson shifted a little, holding the condom so he could carefully withdraw, but he didn't move from the couch right away, and neither did Chloe. Now that the fury of sex was over, she could truly take him in, his amazing body, his tight muscles and intriguing tattoos.

"What does this mean?" she asked, as she traced the dark looped design around his shoulder. It held the hint of a head of a dragon.

"It's a Celtic symbol for dragon," he said. "My father was part Irish and English, and Drake, our family name, means dragon…or snake, depending."

Chloe giggled a little. "You certainly have an impressive snake," she joked.

He laughed as well. "I don't think that's what the ancestors necessarily had in mind."

"Well, an apt name anyway."

"Dad had a dragon tattoo as well, a small one, on his upper biceps. Got it when he joined the navy. I got mine when I turned eighteen. You could say it's a Drake family tradition." He hugged her a little closer and she snuggled in, their body a tangle of limbs on his couch. "Someday maybe my son will have one, too. Or daughter."

"So you want a family?"

"If I find the right girl," he said. But the way he looked at her now with his sharp blue eyes, she thought he might mean she had a fighting chance. "Do you want a family?"

"It's all I've ever really wanted, but…" She thought of Kevin. "It has to be the right person. Someone who'll be a good dad." *Someone who loves me.*

"Fair enough." Jackson glanced down at his belly

and his now-sleeping member. "Well, let me take care of this."

He rolled off the condom and headed to the bathroom. Seconds later, she heard a telltale flush. She remembered his ex, the girlfriend who tried to impregnate herself. She wondered if he now flushed all his condoms for fear of it happening again.

Chloe bit her lip. He didn't trust her. But why would he? They'd only known each other a short time. Still, it bothered her slightly. She wondered why. With him gone, she felt exposed on the couch, more naked than naked. She glanced at the open windows that stared up to her building and saw another light behind mostly closed blinds flicker off. She couldn't see any faces at the windows, and the blinds seemed drawn. Maybe no one had seen them. Maybe everyone had. Who knew?

Still, she realized how reckless she'd been. Now, without Jackson here, she felt a bit vulnerable and scrambled to put on her clothes. She laughed a little to herself. *When have I ever been that bold? Never.* But with Jackson, sex was just…different. Jackson could take her anytime, anyplace, she thought. A body like that. A man who knew what he wanted and wasn't afraid to get it. A man who seemed to be born to pleasure a woman. Why wouldn't she want people to see? Yes, she'd do it all over again, open windows and all. She realized that most of the other men she'd been with had been shier than she was about sex, more conservative, definitely. Jackson wasn't that. He was liberated, out in the open, bold. She liked that. She liked that quite a lot. She remembered how reserved Kevin had been, how he'd insisted on the lights being dim before going at it. She wasn't sure if that was because he was really timid or if it was because he wanted to imagine he was having sex with someone else. Either way, she realized how insecure Kevin had been in all ways. How truly confident Jackson was.

As she stared at the closed bathroom door, his phone, sitting on the end table, dinged. She hadn't meant to look, but then, it was *right* there. Staring her in the face: a message from Annaliese.

Need your glorious cock. Tonight.

Chloe's stomach tightened. Gorgeous Annaliese, from last night. Texting him at nearly midnight. Booty call. Would he take it? She almost wanted to lunge at his phone, delete the message. She glanced at the closed bathroom door. Would he catch her if she did? No, she couldn't do that. It was an invasion of his privacy, and besides, she'd come into this with her eyes open—literally. She'd seen him fuck Annaliese the night before. But two nights in a row? That seemed like an awful lot of benefits for just friends. She shoved the nagging doubt away.

No, she didn't think he'd lied to her.

Then his phone binged again.

I won't look, Chloe told herself. *I won't...*

"Want to take a shower with me?" Jackson called

from the closed door of the bathroom. She nearly jumped out of her skin, her heart thudding.

"One sec," she shouted back.

She couldn't help it. She had to look. The text would disappear soon, behind the pass code of his phone. She glanced at the screen. His phone now showed a text from someone else. Someone named Laurie.

I miss you. Can I come over?

Her whole body ran cold. Who was Laurie?

Remember, he told you: friends...with benefits. Chloe knew he had more than one, so why did it bother her to see the evidence?

Then a picture arrived, a headless shot of...bare breasts, nipples puckered, standing at attention. Followed by a full-frontal shot, showing her hairless mound, pink lips spread ever so slightly, an invitation.

She stood up, mind whirling. She *knew* this about Jackson. He'd been more than up-front with her. Hell, she'd *seen* him with another woman, and yet all the women on his phone just made her feel dizzy. A little bit sick. Was she going to be another willing *friend*, another benefit? Another in a long line of women desperate for his attention?

And why did she care? Then again, she thought how amazing the sex had been. She could already feel herself growing attached, wanting Jackson in a way she shouldn't. Because he wasn't hers. Probably would never be hers.

"Chloe?" Jackson asked, from the door of the bathroom.

Chloe jumped back from the end table, terrified to be caught looking at his phone. "Actually, I've got an early-morning meeting tomorrow," she lied. "Probably should go."

This is best. Get out before you're in too deep. Before you get too attached.

"Are you sure?" Jackson hesitated.

Chloe hated lying to him. *Just tell him you saw that stuff on his phone. Just freakin' tell him.* But she froze. Why wouldn't the words come?

"Chloe," Jackson said, moving so he stood between her and the door, "I want you to stay."

Her head shot up, and she met his blue gaze, serious, unwavering.

"I—I can't," she said, and went around him, heading for the staircase.

"Why?"

"I thought I could do this. The friends and benefits thing," she said to him. "But I don't think I can. I think I'm… I'm looking for something more serious." There, she'd said it. This was what made the phone messages so hard to take. Sure, she'd fallen into Jackson's arms easily, but she also knew herself well enough to know she wanted more of a connection with him. She wanted something deeper. She couldn't just be one of the rotating faces on his phone. She never wanted to feel like she felt with Kevin: as an afterthought.

"Chloe…"

"No." She shook her head and gave him a weak smile. "No, I mean, don't change you, okay? I'm not going to ask you to give up something you don't want to give up. We had a nice time tonight. I just don't want to go on if it's not…well, something more."

"Let me walk you home," he said, reaching for his pants.

"No. That's okay," she said. She hurriedly grabbed her bag, skipped down the stairs and out the alley, terrified he'd come after her. Terrified that he wouldn't. She glanced up and saw Jackson standing up in his living room, staring down at her through the open window.

Better this way, she thought. Yet why didn't it feel like the right thing to do?

CHAPTER EIGHT

JACKSON DIDN'T KNOW what happened. One minute, he was having the best sex of his life and the next minute, Chloe was running out of his place like it was on fire. He watched as she ducked inside her building on the other side of the lit alley and then he waited, staring at her windows. Eventually, a light came on, but her blinds never came up. At least she was home safe. But what had happened?

He yanked on some shorts and grabbed a beer from his fridge just as his phone dinged.

That was when he realized he had a ton of messages. In an instant, he knew what had happened. Annaliese and Laurie had happened.

Dammit.

Now he got it. Her speech about the friends and benefits. Did he want her as just one more woman in his phone? He wasn't sure. Maybe. Maybe not.

But what he did know was that she'd be at the top of his list. He'd never answer their invitations, not with Chloe in his bed. He found it ironic that usually he was the one shooing women out the door. Now the one he finally wanted to stay fled before he had a chance to convince her she should sleep over. Chloe just felt…different from the others. And he felt differently about her. He'd meant what he'd said about ditching the other women if the right one came into his life, and there was a chance Chloe was the one. She intrigued him in a way he hadn't been intrigued… maybe ever. He also had to admit he liked the fire of her standing up for her convictions, her needs. She'd told him that she wanted more. Like him, she wasn't going to be pushed around. He respected that.

He glanced at Laurie's X-rated texts and deleted them. Honestly, what did his ex think? He'd see her naked and forget all the betrayal? Men were simple creatures, but not *that* simple. He decided to ignore her as he usually did. He still couldn't get the image of her trying to impregnate herself out of his head. She'd said she'd loved him, but really, all she wanted was a paycheck. He watched Chloe's light click off. Was she going to bed? She should be beside him, sleeping.

I'm outside your place.

This made him back away from his window, dread dragging at him. Was she here? Jackson went inside, to his buzzer, where he could also see all views of the outside of his building through closed-circuit TV. He checked all the entrances, but saw no sign of Laurie. Then he remembered: she only knew his old address, the one on North Avenue.

I'm buzzing. Why aren't you answering? I need to talk to you.

This had to stop. He imagined her waking up his neighbors. Or the lawyer who'd bought his new place.

We're done, Laurie. I told you. We're over.

He waited, but didn't get a response. Thank goodness. He thought of Chloe once more. Would she end up just like Laurie? Crazed by all the extra zeros in his bank account? This was why it was just simpler to keep it about sex, he thought. And if everybody knew up-front it was just about sex, then nobody got too attached—either to him *or* to his money.

Honestly, he'd never truly been comfortable with the wealth he'd accumulated in a relatively short time.

He texted Chloe, hoping to smooth the waters.

Had a great time with you. Mean it. Would like to see you again.

She didn't respond. He felt a little disappointment in his stomach, but then that was replaced by determination. He wasn't done with Chloe Park. Not yet.

Now wide-awake, he headed to his laptop to check in on work and found an email from Hailey. Kent had countered his offer with another for Chloe's building. It was as outrageous as he thought it would be, with at least one more zero on the end than it merited.

He instructed Hailey to send the man a counteroffer: his price, minus two zeros. After that, still feeling awake, he headed to his wood workshop downstairs and decided to work a little more on his new project, an ornate bar for his house. Even as he put his hands to work, his mind whirled with thoughts of Chloe. For the first time in a long time, a woman occupied his thoughts. Usually he didn't give Annaliese, or any of his other friends with benefits, another thought after a tryst, but now his head was full of images of Chloe's dark eyes. The way she'd come with such an unbridled passion. The way she'd stood in his living room and demanded respect. He might even love that even more. He wanted to see her again. He needed to see her again.

As he molded the wood in his hands, he thought about her soft body, about her tight center. Getting a taste only made him want her more. He'd have to find a way to satisfy that need. He'd figure out a way to see her.

"Well, I'm proud of you, pumpkin, for getting out there." Ryan sat opposite Chloe in one of their favorite lunch spots in Old Town two days later. He wore a crisp plaid button-down short-sleeved shirt and khakis, his standard business-casual fare. He worked as a buyer for a retail chain and was on his lunch hour. Chloe pushed around the kale salad on her plate, feeling a bit despondent. Ryan had ordered a BLT, which he'd mostly devoured.

"Yeah, I guess." Chloe wasn't so sure. Jackson had sent her a sweet text, but she hadn't responded. Not yet. She wasn't certain what she wanted to say. Sometimes she felt completely in control, adult about it, and philosophical. Jackson had broken no promises. He'd offered her white-hot, commitment-free sex, and that was what he'd delivered, and yet at other times she felt like a middle-schooler who'd been let down by a crush. "I don't usually jump into a man's bed on the *first* date."

"Oh. Right. You have your three-date rule." Ryan rolled his eyes to show what he thought of that. He was clean shaven, and wore his perfectly coiffed hair long on top and short on the sides. His dark eyes studied Chloe.

"Hey! I've got *standards*."

"I know! I'm kidding. So he must've been hot if you junked your three-date rule." Ryan popped a small french fry in his mouth.

"Beyond hot." That was the understatement of the year. Their sex might just fuel her alone-time fantasies for weeks to come. Even now, thinking about Jackson's strong hands and…massive self made her belly grow warm.

"So, I get you want more. But how about just be Buddhist about it. Live in the moment, you know? He said he *might* be into something more serious."

"But the women on his phone… I just don't know if I can hang in there, compete with them."

"You don't know until you try." He dipped a

french fry in ketchup, swirling it around at the edge of his plate.

"You think I should see him again." Chloe had her doubts. To her, he seemed like the poster child of a toxic bachelor, the kind that would just toy with her and then eventually break her heart. Like Kevin.

"I think you want to see him again." Ryan quirked an eyebrow, and even she couldn't argue with truth.

Chloe glanced down at her plate. "Yes, of course I do, but I think that's a mistake. Not if he doesn't want what I want."

Ryan's eyes grew wide. "Tell me again how seeing a gorgeous rich man is a mistake? This I have to hear."

"Because I'm just a number, one more willing woman in his phone. It feels…not so good. It's Kevin all over again. And I *swore* I'd never do Kevin." Chloe pushed around the remains of her salad, her appetite whittling even further as her stomach tightened when she remembered the missives on the phone, the gorgeous pictures of naked women. How could she compete with a torrent of willing women? And he'd told her he preferred no strings. That's not what she wanted. Not at all.

"First of all, he's not like Kevin," Ryan said, taking a drink of water. "Kevin was a rich poser, but this guy really is rich."

Chloe laughed a little. "Not funny," she protested. "I didn't care about Kevin's money. It was the fact that he couldn't keep his dick in his pants."

"Right, and about that. Jackson was up-front with you about the other women. He also told you he'd tell them all to take a hike for the right woman, didn't he?"

"I don't want to put pressure on him to do that. Either he does it or not, but I shouldn't have to ask him." Chloe felt like the man ought to volunteer.

"It's your job to elbow the competition out of the way, girl!" Ryan took a small bite of his sandwich. Sunlight filtered through their sidewalk-side window as pedestrians streamed by. Chloe absently watched a woman walk her tiny dog down the sidewalk and sighed.

"Roller-derby dating isn't my style, and I know myself well enough to know that I don't want to be in a catfight over a man who doesn't even *want* what I want." Chloe shrugged one shoulder. "It's just a recipe for disaster. So, I see him again, and we have more awesome sex, and then what? I'm just going to have my heart destroyed—again." She thought about him flushing the condom. One day she wanted a baby, didn't she? Marriage and the whole nine yards. He wasn't in a position to trust anyone, he'd said so, and maybe he'd never be. "Besides, you should've seen those women. They're gorgeous."

Ryan fixed her with a steady, brown-eyed gaze. "So are you, sweetheart."

"Pffft. You have to say that because you're my friend." Chloe exhaled a frustrated breath. She glanced down at her slouchy tee and gym shorts. She wasn't even wearing any makeup today.

"No, actually, if you weren't gorgeous, I'd simply change the subject—awkwardly, and talk about how the Cubs are doing." Ryan grinned. "Besides, you told me that he got all hot and bothered when you saw him with what's-her-name?"

"Annaliese."

"Right. Her. So maybe what's making you so jealous is also making you *attracted* to the man at the same time. Sex is complicated, and often contradictory. We want what we don't want most of the time." Ryan popped a french fry in his mouth. "But I think you're wise. You know what it is you want. But you're assuming you also know what he wants. You don't know for sure. Maybe you ought to let it play out a bit, see how you feel."

"You mean sleep with him some more and then see if he commits? But how can I compete with all those other women?"

Ryan nodded, slowly. "Because you're amazing. Besides, think of all that amazing man meat you get to enjoy until then. Oh, and maybe he'll take you to Girl & the Goat. Or—even better—Alinea."

Those were Chicago's swankiest restaurants, where a tab for two might easily cost hundreds of dollars.

Chloe barked a laugh, and a few of the other patrons turned to stare. "You're awful."

"I'm just honest."

Her cell phone lit up then. It was an incoming message from Jackson.

I want to see you. You free tomorrow?

At the mere sight of his name on her screen, Chloe felt her body react. Yes, how she did want to ride—er, see—him again. There was no question of that.

"Who is it? Is it him?" Ryan leaned forward, eager. She showed him the screen.

"Looks like someone is getting lucky," exclaimed Ryan, reading her phone from across their small table. "Oh...*my*." He raised his eyebrows, meaning clear. "What are you going to do?"

"I don't think I should see him."

"Why?"

"Because I'll get naked again, *that's* why." Chloe knew her self-control was nil when she was with him.

"And that's wrong how?"

"Because I'll get naked, and then I'll fall in love. It only takes two times. Maybe three for me." Chloe shrugged. She knew herself. She wished she could have tons of amazing sex and not get involved, but her emotions just wouldn't be kept at bay. And she was already too far along in falling for Jackson, anyhow.

Ryan shook his head. "You straight girls are a trip."

Chloe laughed. "Please. You're worse than me. You were picking out wedding invitations for Brendan two days after you met him."

Ryan barked a laugh. "I hate that you remember things. Correctly. It's one of your worst qualities." Ryan gave her an exaggerated eye roll. "Okay, fine, so I'm a romantic at heart. You got me. But for the record, Brendan and I had done it *at least* five times by then. Maybe six."

Chloe laughed. "Fair enough."

Ryan chewed thoughtfully. "You told him you want something more serious, and he's asking you out, so why not wait and see if he offers it?"

"You think?" Chloe wasn't sure. She thought about all those pictures on his phone. Yes, attraction was complicated, but what about her own self-respect?

I don't think that's a good idea, she responded.

"I can't believe you just turned him down!" Ryan cried, looking at the phone. "How do you know how serious he is—or isn't—until you give him a try?"

"That's the problem. I already tried him. And I like him. Too much."

Another message came through.

I think we should talk.

"Talk?" Chloe echoed. "About...?"

"Maybe the man is going to give you what you want." Ryan took a sip of water, swallowing down a bite of sandwich.

Chloe scoffed. "You think he's going to want an exclusive relationship with me?"

"Maybe. He said he wants to talk. You know how

much guys hate to talk." Ryan bit into another fry. Chloe studied the phone in her hand.

"But I literally already gave the milk away for free…"

"Maybe he *really* likes your milk, honey." Ryan laughed a little at his own joke.

I want to talk. I also need a date today. I'm throwing a party for my employees. Wanted to know if you'd be my plus-one? We can talk after. I promise.

"Well, now," Ryan said, reading the screen. "Bringing you as a plus-one to anything doesn't sound like a man who's planning to relegate you to the role of friends with benefits."

A little bit of hope sprang up in Chloe's chest. "Do you think so?"

"Definitely."

The party was held at the horse track, in the elite private club rooms far above the race. For an invitation to Arlington Park, Chloe figured a sundress would do, but Ryan had warned her that Drake Properties threw fancy parties. She pulled on strappy stilettos to make the easy sundress more formal.

She wondered what it meant that he was bringing her as his date. Was Ryan right? Was he more serious about her than the other women? Then again, she also told herself, what did *she* even know about Jackson Drake? He had money and he had abs and…a member that wouldn't quit. But shouldn't *she* slow down and get to know *him*, too? She'd go on this date, hear what he had to say, and then make up her mind. If he wasn't prepared to give her what she needed, she'd walk. She wasn't about to start up a relationship with another Kevin.

She took a deep breath as she touched up her makeup, wondering if her sleeveless, halter-like sundress was too revealing. It was a lower-cut neckline than she usually wore, but Jackson was making her braver than her normal self. Maybe that's one of the reasons she was drawn to him. He was bold and he made her feel bolder, too. Dangerous, that's exactly what he was. Part of her couldn't resist playing with fire. After all, she'd never felt so brazen before, never felt so exposed *and* so seen.

Looking in the mirror, at her dark hair up in a low ponytail, she felt passable, maybe more than that, now that she was wearing dark eyeliner that highlighted her nearly black eyes. Plus, she couldn't help think they did have a connection somehow. The passion she'd felt wasn't something that came along every day, and part of her thought Jackson must feel it, too.

Jackson's car roared in the alley, the amazing engine a burst of just-bridled power. Chloe went to the window and saw him behind his familiar Maserati. The hood gleamed in the sunlight, all expensive lines, chrome and brand-new leather seats. The afternoon was a rare seventy-five degrees, a perfect Chicago summer's day, with a breeze off Lake Michigan that dropped the temperature a few degrees. Jackson wore a collared shirt and a tight mesh fedora, which somehow he made look slightly dangerous.

"Nice hat," she said, nodding her approval.

"It's the thing to wear to the racetrack, so I hear." She was barely paying attention to what he said as she was too busy following the lines of his tattoo, just visible from the open collar of his shirt. God, the man was all sex and danger.

He left the car and sauntered over to her as his eyes swept her outfit. "Hey, sexy," he purred, and then pulled her close. She bent her head, and he laid a soft kiss on her lips. His blond goatee brushed her chin and she felt a shiver of pure pleasure run down her back. Her body responded to him so instinctively. Warning bells went off in the back of her mind. If she wasn't careful, she'd wind up falling for him. Hard.

If she hadn't already.

"Hey," she said, pulling back, his ice-blue eyes studying her. God, did she love those eyes. She could stare at them forever. No—the talk. Remember! They needed to talk first.

"So…you wanted to talk?" Chloe was proud of bringing it up right away. She wasn't going to let him off the hook.

"After the party, okay?" he said.

"Okay," she agreed, reluctantly.

Jackson pulled the passenger-side door open, and she slid into the low-set caramel-colored leather.

"How many cars do you have?" she teased as he rounded the car and headed to the driver's side.

"Not enough," he said, and grinned. He slid into the driver's seat, and the car roared to life, and soon, he'd swung them out of the alley and into traffic.

She'd never been to Arlington Park before, and about forty minutes later, as they pulled into the special parking near the track, she could hear the sounds of fans cheering the races that had only just begun. Jackson took Chloe by the hand and led her to a private elevator, where nearby, men and women casually stood in groups talking, all of them dressed elegantly, the women wearing expensive hats. She was beginning to think this was more Kentucky Derby than casual outing, and suddenly even her long sundress and strappy stilettos didn't seem dressy enough.

"Should I have worn a hat?" she asked as they stepped inside the elevator.

"You're perfect just the way you are," Jackson growled, knocking his own fedora down a little so it covered his blue eyes. With his goatee and sharp, rugged good looks, he seemed too primal for the dark suit jacket he'd slung over the oxford button-down he wore, the expensive wing tips on his feet.

As the elevator doors shut, Jackson pulled her into his arms and kissed the life out of her, his tongue mingling with hers. He tasted like peppermint, the gum he'd been chewing, yet it was the firmness of his chest and abs pressed against hers that reminded her that kissing wasn't the only thing he did well. She had a sudden urge to explore the front of his pants but then stopped herself. The elevator was opening any minute. That was when Jackson's hands moved downward and he possessively cupped her backside, pulling her to him so their groins met. She felt the stirrings of his massive size there and instantly felt dampness between her legs. Suddenly, she didn't much want to watch the horses race. She'd much rather hit Stop on this elevator and see where the next moments took them.

The elevator doors slid open then, and cool air-conditioning hit them.

"Welcome to the Governor's Room," he said, and held the doors open as she walked off the elevator onto thick blue carpet. A wall of windows met her, and she realized she was at the top of the racetrack, looking down on the dirt circle where horses gathered at the starting gate for the next race.

Waiters in suits carried champagne on trays, and already people milled about the expansive private room, painted a pristine white, with large, expensive light fixtures hanging from the ceiling, and a long granite-topped counter filled with every kind of fine food imaginable. A waiter offered her a glass of champagne, but Jackson smoothly intervened.

"Get the lady and me some of my private select bourbon on the rocks, please," he said, and grinned at Chloe. "I remembered you weren't a bubbles kind of girl."

"You get points."

"I hope so." The way he was looking at her now, Chloe felt like the only woman in the world. She wished she always felt that way, and then immediately tried to banish the negative thought. *You're here with an amazing man, on an amazing date. Do what Ryan said. Live in the moment.*

The waiter returned with two amber-colored drinks and handed them to Chloe and Jackson. Jackson clinked his glass against hers. "To the most beautiful woman in this room," he said, and she felt red-hot heat creep around her ears. She certainly wasn't the most beautiful woman in the room, that was for sure. The room was crawling with what Chloe could only guess were the prettiest women in Chicago. Some looked familiar, like they might be from *Chicago Fire*. Anything was possible. As Chloe sipped on her delicious bourbon, she watched Jackson as he took in the crowd. It wasn't long before a beautiful, statuesque blonde approached them.

"So glad you could make it, sir," she said, bending her head slightly in formality. "And who's your lovely date?"

Chloe stared at the woman, amazed at the fact that she could literally see no pores on the woman's face. Her skin was perfection itself, and she was thin, tall and striking. She felt her gut tighten in jealousy. She was short, curvy and dark, not tall, lithe and model-like.

"Hailey, this is Chloe. Chloe, Hailey. She's my right brain at work. The world's best executive assistant."

"Pleasure to meet you," Hailey said, sounding genuine as she shook Chloe's hand. Chloe wondered if the two slept together. She also wondered if she'd *always* suspect that when Jackson introduced her to a good-looking woman. Looking around at the Drake Properties party, she realized there were desperately few ugly people in the room. She wondered if Jackson did that on purpose. Or maybe beautiful people just sold more real estate. Whatever the case, it was hard not to feel intimidated.

"You, too," Chloe said, inspecting Hailey's amazing, British-royalty-wedding-worthy hat. "I should've worn a hat."

"Hats optional, don't worry," Hailey said, giving her a genuinely affectionate grin. Chloe warmed to the gorgeous blonde, suddenly grateful for her friendly smile. "But if you really want one, I have a few stashed away, just in case. We've got clients coming as well as agents, and my motto is always be prepared."

"That's why she's the best assistant in the world." Jackson said it as a matter of fact, and Chloe noticed there wasn't any flirting in his tone. No, the two didn't have benefits, she decided. Would she be worried about every woman he knew?

"You don't mind if I borrow one?" Chloe was feeling decidedly underdressed. It's not like she had fancy hats lying around her closet at home. Clearly, she wasn't used to private box parties at horse race-tracks. But then, why would she be?

This is how the other half lives, she thought. *Or scratch that, the other 1 percent.*

Chloe followed Hailey into a large walk-in coat closet, and Hailey reached up for a fabric crate. "I think I know the perfect one. It'll match your dress perfectly. By the way, lovely dress. Where did you get it?"

"On sale. Nordstrom Rack," Chloe said, and then immediately cringed as she glanced at Hailey's Christian Louboutin pumps that cost more than her whole outfit, times three.

"I love bargains," Hailey said, being kind. Chloe had no idea what Hailey made as Jackson's assistant, but judging by her clothes, her salary had more zeros than Chloe's. Hailey pulled out a floppy felt camel-colored hat that did manage to go perfectly with her strawberry-and-cream-striped dress.

"What's it like? Working for Jackson?" Chloe asked, curious, as she took the hat, studying it and trying to figure out which was the front and which end was the back.

"Oh, he's an amazing boss. Fair, generous and so very smart. I've learned so much from him. He's caring, too. He stood up at my wedding to my wife last summer." She emphasized the word *wife*, and realization dawned on Chloe.

"Your wife?" Well then, there was *definitely* nothing going on between her and Jackson. She felt a rush of relief flood her. "Congratulations!"

Hailey smiled. "Thank you. We're very happy." She beamed, and Chloe perched the hat on her head and glanced at the long mirror hanging on the back of the door. She had to admit, the hat did complete the ensemble. She almost looked as sophisticated, and rich, as the rest of the party.

"You look…great!" Hailey chirped. She studied Chloe a beat. "You know, it's none of my business, but…"

Chloe paused, wondering if this was when Hailey told her that she didn't stand a chance against his legions of adoring naked fans, all the willing women in his phone.

"Well, I think you two must be serious because Jackson never brings a date to these things." Hailey stared at Chloe. "How long have you two been…"

Uh, two days.

"Not long," Chloe said, trying to process the fact that Jackson's assistant was telling her that despite the many women she knew were waiting in his phone, he usually preferred to go stag to company events.

"Well, I'm very glad to meet you, because we always say Jackson needs to date more. We never see any serious girlfriends."

"Never?" Chloe thought about all his friends with benefits, and realized how he must keep those secret from work. Or maybe, there weren't as many women as she thought. Either way, she couldn't help feeling a bit special. He was taking her to a work event. Maybe she was *not* just another friend with benefits?

"Seriously, we never get to meet anyone he dates, so he must think you're special. He wouldn't bring you here if he didn't." Hailey beamed at Chloe, and Chloe couldn't help but beam back. Was that true?

Hailey straightened Chloe's hat a bit. "I've known him for years," she continued. "If he's letting *me* meet you, and all his other employees, then that is something. Trust me."

Chloe's heart ticked up. She liked that revelation a little too much. *Could just be gossip from an assistant, nothing more*, she warned herself.

"Knock, knock." Jackson stood at the coat closet door, resting against the doorjamb, all six foot two inches of him. His own straw fedora was tilted dangerously down over his sharp blue eyes. He held both their drinks in his hands. "I like the hat," he said, handing her the drink he'd been holding for her. He glanced at Hailey, a subtle exchange between boss and employee.

"My work is done here," Hailey exclaimed. "I'll see you two out there." She scooted past Jackson, leaving the two alone in the coatroom. Jackson put his drink down on one of the open cubbies in the closet.

Jackson took a step closer, moving the brim of Chloe's hat back a bit. She craned her neck as his blue eyes fixed on hers, the oversize ice cube clinking the side of her glass.

"You look good enough to eat," he said, voice a low hum in her ears.

Chloe heard the chatter from the party outside, the coatroom door ajar, but all that didn't seem to matter as Jackson took another step closer. He trailed a single finger down the neckline of her dress, his finger caressing the hint of cleavage there. She sucked in a breath and held it. She'd promised herself that she'd keep her clothes on until they talked, but now, standing before Jackson, she realized the temptation might be too great for her to resist. Could she tell this amazing man no? Her body sure as hell didn't want to.

"I want you," Jackson said, gaze never leaving her face.

"Right now?" Chloe squeaked, glancing back at the open door.

A daring smile crossed his face. "Right now, right here."

CHAPTER NINE

JACKSON LEANED IN and took her drink from her hand. The fact was, he wanted her, badly, and was tired of fighting the urge to keep his hands off her. Yes, they were at a work function, but that didn't curb his libido at all. There was something about Chloe that just got under his skin, bypassed all logic circuitry of his brain. He wasn't sure what it was, or how it had come over him so quickly, but she was different. Maybe it was her boldness? He stepped closer, his lips close to touching hers, when his phone rang, interrupting the moment. He pulled it out of his pocket and saw Laurie's name there. Damn that woman! He silenced his phone and put it back in his pocket.

"You sure you don't need to get that?" she asked him, dark eyes wide.

"I'm sure." More than sure.

Then Chloe's own phone dinged. She dug it out of her bag, glanced at the screen and then quickly put the phone away. Did she have suitors, too? His stomach knotted a little. What if she had an untold number of men on her phone, pinging her all the time? He should've guessed she had. After all, she was gorgeous, whip smart and funny. Why wouldn't she be pursued? If he was interested, others would be, too.

Somehow, the thought made him want her even more. He took a step forward, keeping his back to the door as he leaned in and kissed her, a feather-soft kiss. Even with that light touch, he felt his own body respond to hers, stiffening with want. He almost didn't care about the party outside the open door. He knew he shouldn't take this any further, and yet part of him wanted to.

Then he heard the distinct sound of a man clearing his throat. Chloe jumped a mile, but Jackson just slowly drew back, a ripple of frustration running through him as he turned to address the intruder, a man wearing a polo and khakis, a cocktail in hand.

Kent.

What was he doing here? He wasn't a Drake Properties employee.

"Jackson! Been looking all over for you... Sorry, didn't mean to interrupt."

Jackson knew Kent absolutely intended to interrupt. The man had the worst timing. Also, he didn't like the way Kent was looking at Chloe. Correction: looking at her chest.

"Kent," Jackson said, voice slightly strained. "I wasn't aware...you were coming." *Or that you were invited. Actually, I know you weren't.*

"Oh, I just happened to be in the suite next door

with friends, and saw the Drake Properties party sign. Figured I'd drop in and say hello."

Jackson wished the man would drop himself off the balcony.

"You've said it, and now…"

"Aren't you going to introduce me to this gorgeous little lady?" Kent grinned, but he still stared at Chloe's chest. If he kept doing that, Jackson would have to do something about it.

"Kent Roberts, this is Chloe Park. My *date*." He said the word emphatically, so Kent would have no misconceptions. Chloe was *his* date. Not up for flirting with the likes of him.

"Yes! Wanted to let you know I got your offer. Maybe we could meet in the middle?"

"Let's talk about it—Monday," Jackson said, cutting him off and not really caring if he sounded rude. Kent was overstepping his bounds. The last thing he needed at the moment was an open discussion of how he planned to buy Chloe's building.

He turned to Chloe. "Are you feeling hungry? Maybe you'd like a bit to eat?"

She nodded, and he led her past Kent into the party, where dozens of his own agents and workers were already mingling, cocktails in hand. Kent trailed behind them, annoyingly close, and Jackson made a mental note to try to lose him as soon as possible. Then he saw Hailey talking with the head of security, frowning. He knew something was up even before she made eye contact with him across the room and gave him a subtle head nod.

He squeezed Chloe's elbow as they reached the buffet and she grabbed a golden-rimmed plate. "I'll be right back," he said, voice low.

Chloe glanced up at him.

"Everything okay?" she asked.

"I just need to check on something," he added, and retreated, meeting Hailey across the room with three long strides.

"What's the matter?" he asked, knowing by the look on her face something wasn't quite right. He kept his voice low enough that it didn't rise above the general hum of conversation around them.

Hailey looked uncharacteristically uncomfortable. Whatever she had to tell him, she didn't want to deliver bad news. "Do you know a woman named Laurie?"

Instantly, Jackson felt a weight on his shoulders.

"Unfortunately. We dated. Briefly." He never should've started dating her at all, he thought.

"Well, she's at the main gate. Demanding to see you." Hailey bit her lip, looking extremely uncomfortable as she shifted from one foot to the other, her own gaze hesitant to meet his.

Jackson shook his head. "I broke things off with her, but she's not taking no for an answer." He sighed. "Please have security escort her off the premises. She is not welcome here."

Hailey nodded quickly. "Yes, sir."

Jackson hated that Laurie had made his personal life public, especially since he'd made it more than clear that they were done. He wondered briefly if he ought to get his attorney involved, get a restraining order.

"Oh, and Hailey," Jackson said, almost as an afterthought. "Call my attorney on Monday, would you? I'd like to talk to her." Best to nip this in the bud. He couldn't have a crazy, money-obsessed ex showing up at his home and business. He needed advice on what to do, maybe even the steps to getting a restraining order.

Hailey nodded quickly. "Yes, sir."

Jackson turned then and saw that Kent had maneuvered Chloe into a corner. She was holding on to an appetizer plate like a shield, the tiny sliver of china only thing between her and him. He was talking emphatically about something, and clearly invading her personal space. He frowned. He didn't like Kent making a move on his date. He had his hand on her *elbow*. She wasn't entirely resisting him, either. It was true Kent was a decent-looking guy, and his money made him even more attractive. He felt a flare of jealousy even as his rational mind told him that Chloe wasn't doing anything more than being polite.

He crossed the room in quick, purposeful strides and caught the tail end of their conversation, which had something to do with Kent's yacht.

"Sorry about that," Jackson told Chloe. "Just a little work emergency." He was glad to see that Chloe looked happy—and relieved—to see him.

"No worries," Kent said, grinning like a cat who'd eaten a canary. "I was just telling Chloe that she was welcome aboard my yacht anytime. We're sailing to Greece this year."

"Oh?" Jackson wished the man would set sail *right now.* "Is that because you raised rents in Pilsen this year?" Pilsen was one of Chicago's eclectic neighborhoods, part hipster, with a heavy Latino influence, and a mix of housing. Kent owned condos near the Thalia concert hall, but he was notorious for his high rents and his lack of fixing real problems, like a back staircase that collapsed last summer.

Kent frowned at the reference.

"Well, it was good to see you, Kent, but if you'll excuse us?" Jackson put his hand on the small of Chloe's back and led her away from the slumlord. Jackson maneuvered Chloe to the other end of the private room, closer to the windows facing out to the racetrack. "Tell me you aren't going to go on his yacht."

"Him? I don't think I'd want to be anywhere near him," Chloe declared. "I only talked to him five minutes, and all he wanted to talk about was himself."

Jackson chuckled a little. "It's his favorite subject."

"But he did say he had a private chef," Chloe teased, meeting his gaze.

"I'll cook for you as long as you stay away from

him." Jackson glanced at Kent across the room. The man lacked a moral compass, and it was all about greed for him. How much he could make, and how hard he could screw others out of a hard-earned dollar. That was what he liked the most about the real estate business.

"Is that a promise?" Chloe lifted her face, her floppy hat falling back a bit, so that her dark eyes shone in the sunlight, making them look a lighter brown, almost golden. Jackson felt his need for her rise again.

"Yes," he said, voice a little huskier than usual. "I want to kiss you again."

Chloe's lips parted. "Here?" She glanced around at the crowded party, and Jackson realized she had a point. Making out with his date in front of his employees probably wasn't the smartest idea. He glanced over at the nearby coatroom, but saw a few people hanging by the door. That venue was out. He gently took her hand.

"Feel like exploring?" he asked.

A slow grin broke out across her face. "Sure," she said, as if she'd been made his partner in crime.

He led her out of the party room. Several of the suites were taken, but at the end of the long carpeted hallway, they found an empty room. He pulled her inside and slid the lock into place behind them. He turned to find her studying him with her dark eyes. He glanced at her in her floppy hat and her sexy sundress, which now, in the sunlight, seemed slightly transparent. He could see the outline of her sexy legs as she stood before the sun-drenched windows.

The room was empty, nothing but large blue carpet, a single empty table in the center, and a wall of windows facing the races. Outside, someone fired a starting gun and the horses took off in one of many scheduled races. But Jackson cared only about Chloe at that moment.

"I missed you," he said, realizing that since their one night together, just days ago, he *had* missed her. Ached for her, actually. Since having her in his living room, he wanted nothing more than to get her naked again. He wasn't used to feeling so exposed, so needy. It wasn't like him.

"You've been with me all day."

"Not the way I want to be." He took a step closer and claimed her mouth with his, this time, his hands roving freely down her back as he grabbed her hips and pulled her to him. She arched into him, her mouth opening for him, eager, wet, delicious.

As his tongue explored her mouth, his need grew. He wondered if he'd ever have his fill of her. He was so busy tasting her, pushing his body into hers, that eventually they hit something solid: the glass wall. Her back against it, he trailed kisses down her neck, making her moan with want. God, he loved to make her moan. He wanted to make her do it all day. All night. He could feel her rapid intake of breath as he kissed her neckline, softly licking the delicious vee where her breasts met. He cupped one, felt its heavy weight in his hand. Perfect.

He claimed her mouth once more, and she ran her nails through the back of his hair, laying perfect trails across his scalp. She raised one knee, opening herself to him, as he ran his hand up her thigh, pushing away the fabric until his palm hit bare skin. She was so soft, so perfect there as he held her outer leg and pressed himself against her warmth at her very center. His body screamed with need as the blood rushed to his groin. He wanted her. Now. Here. He didn't care that the room was open, that the wall of windows had no shades. He didn't care if anyone saw them. He reached up and touched the edge of her G-string. The woman wore the sexiest underwear.

It was then he realized that if he moved his hand much farther, he'd show the entire world her G-string since she was pressed against the windows. Not that she seemed to care, but still, he pulled her away from them, retreating back into the empty suite. The closest people were sixty feet down, anyway, in the rows of spectators beneath them. And most of them had their attention fixed on the track. A roar of cheers went up as the horses neared the final turn and the announcer called the lead horses out by name.

Something about the daylight streaming in through the clear windows, the muted roar of the crowd outside, made his heart pound harder.

He pushed her up on the table against the far wall,

keeping his back to the windows, his tongue deep in her mouth. He broke free, breathing ragged.

"Want me to stop?" he asked.

"No," she said, need in her voice. Want.

"I don't have a condom," he managed, realizing that he hadn't planned on ravishing her here, in this suite. Hard disappointment hit him like a fist.

"I don't care," she said, pulling his hands up to her inner thigh. He brushed the thin fabric of the lace there, the only thing between him and her sweet, wet center. It was drenched with her desire, and feeling her white-hot heat for him only made his own groin tighten painfully. He needed to release himself. He needed her. Now. "I… I'm on the Pill," she managed.

"And…I don't have anything," he said, to address the other concern. Safety. "I get checked for STDs every year, and I'm clean."

"Me, too," Chloe murmured, voice low. "I got checked after…my breakup with my ex. All clear."

Was he going to do this? Trust a woman he barely knew? Laurie had said she was on the Pill, too, and then he'd caught her trying to get herself pregnant. Never before in his life had he set cold calculation aside, and he'd certainly never been this careless before. Once again, Chloe seemed to change all the rules. He didn't know how, but she did. For the first time in his life, he felt he could truly trust a woman. He believed her.

She was undoing his pants, freeing him, and he felt the cool air-conditioning on his groin, but it did nothing to drench his pulsating need for her. His mind went blank about anything but her. She wiggled free of her underwear, sliding it down one leg. Her pupils had grown so big her eyes looked nearly black. Yes, she wanted him. Her lips were red and raw from his kisses. How could he say no to this? He couldn't care less about the distant windows behind them, about who might see them together, about the lack of protection. He needed her. He couldn't wait any longer.

He plunged into her, her tight wet center grasping him, and he nearly came inside her right then. God, it had been years since he'd felt a woman like this, bare, no condom, just skin on skin. He'd always been so careful, the first to put up barriers, to prevent pregnancy, to prevent entanglement and other consequences. He'd forgotten how wonderful this was, how much better sex really could be. Or it might be that with Chloe, it just *was* better. And in this moment, he found he didn't care at all about that. Not now. Not when she felt so wonderfully perfect, not when it almost seemed like every second of his life was for this one moment. Inside her. Bare. This was what he was meant to do.

To hell with consequences. He needed her. He needed her just like this.

She clutched at him, muffling her cries. Her face was flushed, and her panting grew. She glanced at him, eyes dilated with pure pleasure.

"Oh, God. I'm going to come," she told him, the

news rippling through him, driving him to grow even harder, his need a throbbing tower. She grabbed his shoulders, and her grip on him grew so tight he thought he would lose it. She came in a rushing spasm that nearly toppled him over the edge. That was what he wanted to do, he realized. He wanted to come in her. He was meant to come in her. This was where he belonged.

He was going to do it. Gush inside her. Deep inside.

Then a sliver of rational thought caught him at the end. What if…she wasn't on the Pill? Or, what if the Pill failed? The frigid thought choked him and at the very last second, he pulled out, spilling himself across her belly in an almost never-ending river. God, so much come, so much come that was meant for her. This was how badly he wanted her, the evidence glistening on her lower abdomen in a shocking streak. He sucked in air, his heart pounding from his climax and from the notion that he'd almost *come inside her.* No condom. Nothing. Never had he been so reckless. It was what the woman did to him.

"I'm…sorry. We shouldn't have done that," he murmured now, feeling contrite. The dangers of that made his mind whirl. Sure, they'd both said they were clean, but he also knew there were still risks. But what scared him most was the hollow disappointment in his chest about not coming inside her. He felt a strange emptiness.

"No. It's okay," she murmured, cheeks flushed with her own come. "I wanted it."

And he did, too. He knew that. Part of him even realized that it had all been worth it: to feel her, all of her eager for him, needing him. Even now, he wanted to feel her again, without barriers, skin on skin. He wanted to be as close as was physically possible. He wondered if his feelings for her bordered on manic.

He took his shirttail and gently wiped his evidence from her stomach.

He felt his groin shiver with renewed life. Did he want to feel her again? Did he want to come in her this time? Yes, he realized with a shock. He did. He'd thought she drained him, and yet now, he almost wanted to see if she could draw more out of him. He knew he wanted to feel her clench him as he came. All of him. At the very deepest point inside her. He imagined all that come inside her, filling her up…and he felt himself begin to harden once more.

He pulled away from her and tucked himself back in, zipping himself up to keep from trying once more. He couldn't afford thoughts like these. Dangerous thoughts. Coming in her? Was he crazy? Was he really ready to trust her so much?

She pulled down her dress and laid a cautious hand on her hair, her attention flickering to the bare windows behind them. Then she shrugged.

"Looks like I've crossed over from voyeur to exhibitionist," she said, and grinned. God, he loved her free spirit, her devil-may-care attitude. She was bold, like he was. He admired that. And it made him think they'd have brave, adventurous children…if they chose to.

"Whatever you are, it's perfect. You're perfect," he said, and meant it. He'd never come that hard for a woman—that much before—that he knew of. He'd never been with a woman who made him feel so on edge, so dangerously close to giving up everything. He felt like he was walking on a tightrope without a net below him, and it felt exhilarating.

Was this what love, true love, felt like?

CHAPTER TEN

CHLOE AND JACKSON returned to the party, and Chloe felt like everyone there knew the two had just had the most incredible sex. She almost thought they should be able to sense it somehow, maybe even smell it on her, as she mingled in the crowd. She felt dirty, but in the best possible way. He put a cocktail in her hand and she sipped at it, feeling the cool orange sweetness of the old-fashioned slide down her throat. She felt jittery, unnerved. She couldn't believe she'd just had sex *in public*, but that she'd also done so without a condom, or even having the talk about whether they were exclusive or not. She almost cursed herself. She'd promised not to get naked, and yet…that's exactly what she'd just done. The man was like walking heroin, though. How could she resist him? Gorgeous, strong and endowed. Oh so endowed.

She glanced at him at her elbow, easily making small talk with a few of his agents, and wondered if he thought she was *that kind of girl*. Honestly, she was never so careless. She'd always used condoms, always did it with the shades (mostly) down,

but something about Jackson just invited her to be...
naughty. She found she liked it. The thrill of it all,
the risk. She felt daring and bold, like the bad girl
she maybe always secretly hoped to be.

It was worse than she had feared when she told
Ryan. Hadn't she said this would happen? That she
would get naked? God, she didn't even wait until
they'd gotten *home* from the party. Inwardly, she
laughed at that. Of course, it's not like she'd ever really been into vanilla sex, but she'd never pushed the
boundaries like this, either. Chloe wondered briefly
what Kevin would think of her now. If *this* bold, daring version of Chloe had been in his bed, maybe he
never would've accidentally called her by a different name.

Was that why she was so determined to take such
risks? Was she proving something to Kevin? To herself? Or was it the allure of Jackson's desire for her?
She'd never felt so wanted, so desired by a man before.
The feeling made all her nerve endings come alive.

Maybe her attraction to him was so strong, she'd
do anything he asked. Strip naked right here in the
middle of this cocktail party and fuck him while
everybody watched. The idea sent a chill down her
spine, and she felt a warmth pool between her legs.
She'd just come with Jackson inside her and now here
she was imagining sex with him again?

She took another slug of her drink. No, she would
have this talk with him, he promised. He said after
the party, and so she'd wait. Just because she'd had

sex with him—again—that didn't change her feelings. She wanted more from him, and if he couldn't
give it to her, she'd leave.

Leave the best sex you've ever had?

Chloe had to shore up her resolve. She had to walk
away if there was no future with Jackson.

Jackson made a joke and the circle around them
laughed. Chloe only half remembered their names,
and it was probably because with Jackson at her elbow,
all she could think of was him: the feel of his bare skin
against hers just seconds ago; him, all of him, inside
her. Was there such a thing as being addicted to a
man? Because she might need rehab. Soon.

She mentally shook herself. At this rate, she was
going to get naked—again—before they got home.
She tried to focus on Jackson, on the conversation at
hand. He was so good to his employees and seemed
to truly care about them. She liked that he wasn't a
standoffish billionaire boss. Everyone felt like they
could approach him and did. She got more than a few
curious stares, and she realized that Hailey had been
right: Jackson didn't bring around many women to
work functions. She made a mental note to ask him
why he'd made an exception.

Then again, after what they'd just done down the
hall, maybe she had her answer.

"We don't have to stay," he said in her ear. "Do
you want to go?"

The last race was about to begin, though the
crowd had thinned out a bit.

"Let's stay for the last race," she said, nodding out to the track. "I haven't even bet yet!"

"Then let's do that." Jackson grinned at her and led her to their own electronic teller near the corner and pulled out ten hundred-dollar bills.

"That's too much!" she cried.

"Which horse do you like?" Jackson asked, making no room for argument. She looked at the various names: Jefferson's Dog, Henry's Folly, Neck and Neck, Recon Elite, Panda Art, Miya Sophia, Sarina Jon.

"I don't know anything about horses," she protested, not sure how this all worked.

"Just pick by the name. That's what I'd do." Jackson grinned.

"Okay…if you're sure…" She studied the list of horses. "I'm going with Miya Sophia. That has a nice ring to it."

"How about for second place and third place?"

"Sarina Jon, and…Panda Art. Why not?" Chloe giggled.

He punched a few options on the touch screen and the computer spit out betting tickets, which he took. "Okay, bets are laid. Now let's go watch." Jackson led her to an open spot near one of the windows, which also had a view of the television coverage. The horses neighed and shook their heads in the race stalls, as their jockeys climbed atop their backs and worked to settle the big beasts. Nearby, women and men crowded the glass, wearing suits and fine dresses and straw hats. Jackson gently clasped her hand as they watched the screens, as the jockeys settled in, readying for the starting gun. She loved the feel of his big, smooth palm pressed against hers, and standing so close to him, she got a whiff of his aftershave, something spicy and sweet all at once. Boy, he smelled good. She found herself leaning into his shoulder, inhaling deeply.

The pop of the starting gun grabbed her attention, and she watched the TV as the horses catapulted out of their pens. Far below them, she couldn't see the actual horses. They were on the other side of the giant stadium, blocked by tents in the middle of the field. Their box had a straight view to the finish. She watched the television as the horses galloped down the dirt track, flinging up bits of mud as the small jockeys steered them around the first bend. Jackson let out a whoop as Miya Sophia burst ahead of the bunch, followed closely by Panda Art and Roblox Elite. Sarina Jon and Neck and Neck lagged in the thick of the pack.

"Go, Panda Art!" Chloe shouted, and had to laugh at how ridiculous that sounded. Still, she squeezed Jackson's hand as she watched Miya Sophia widen her lead, and Sarina Jon broke free of the crowd, inching closer to the front. Neck and Neck was neck and neck with Panda Art. "Come on!" Chloe shouted once more, but Neck and Neck looked like he was losing steam in the last stretch. The horses came thundering down the pass, and now Chloe could see them in real time down the stretch of track beneath their box. The jockeys urged the horses on, but in the end, Miya Sophia won, followed by Sarina Jon and…Neck and Neck. Panda Art couldn't pull out the third-place finish after all.

But Jackson cheered and hugged Chloe. "Two out of three isn't bad. We won a little money," he said.

"Did you win?" Hailey asked them both.

"We won part of our bet," he said. "You?"

"Nope. Lost another dollar!" Hailey said. "Oh, well. It's just not my lucky day. I haven't won any of these races."

Jackson reached in his pocket and handed her a ticket. "We have more than one winning ticket on this race. Here, this is yours." He handed it to her. Chloe wasn't sure what it had won, but Hailey seemed to know since her eyes lit up.

"Sir! Are you sure…?"

"Positive. You take that one."

She clutched the ticket and beamed. "Oh, thank you, sir. Thank you."

"I'll see you on Monday," he said, and took Chloe gently by the crook of her elbow and led her out the door.

"What was that ticket worth?" she asked him.

"It was the marginal winner. So, two thousand dollars?"

Chloe felt her throat go dry. "That's a *marginal* winner? What did *we* win, then?"

"Ten thousand dollars. Give or take. Those were long odds on Miya Sophia. And I happened to add in a ticket that included Neck and Neck in third, too. To hedge our bets. So we got a trifecta."

Chloe felt her head spin. Ten *thousand* dollars? They'd just won...more than two months of her salary. He was so blasé about it, too, but then again, she realized he was flush with cash. He didn't have to worry about which utility bill he'd pay first, not like her. She was suddenly aware of how very different their lifestyles truly were. He thought a five-hundred-dollar bet was nothing more than buying a single lotto ticket, and the prize winnings didn't even faze him.

"Let's go claim our prize," he said as he led her into the now-open elevator.

Chloe looked at Jackson: the handsome, dirty-blond with the tattoos, the goatee and the straw fedora, and wondered if she'd ever get used to the easy way he treated money. Is this why women fell for him? Was it the endless supply of cash? The allure of being taken care of?

The elevator doors dinged open and Jackson went to the cashier, to claim their $10,000 prize. The man ducked into a locked back room, and then he emerged with two thick stacks of hundred-dollar bills tucked in a manila envelope. Jackson thanked him and handed the envelope to her.

"Oh, no. I can't accept this!" She tried to give the money back.

"You picked the horses," he pointed out.

"So? It was your money. I'm not taking this." She stuffed the envelope back into the pocket of his suit jacket. She felt wrong taking the money, even as she knew it would mean unlimited air-conditioning for the summer and she'd completely pay off her Visa, maybe even pay her student loans *ahead* of time. But still. It was too much.

"You should take it," Jackson said, holding out the envelope as they stood in the lobby of the racetrack.

"No." She shook her head firmly. "I'm with you for the *sex*, not your money," she joked.

Jackson threw back his head and laughed at that, and Chloe laughed, too.

"Fine," he said, and tucked the cash back in his jacket pocket. "Then let's get naked again if you're just after me for my body."

She looped her arm through his. "What are we waiting for?"

Back at his apartment, he led her into his dark foyer as he flipped on a light. She'd barely paid attention to the lower two levels the first time at his place, since she'd been in such a rush to get to his living room, the room with the windows that faced her apartment. As they passed the second floor, he flipped the switch and she now saw his workshop clearly. Almost the entire floor was dedicated to his woodworking hobby. He had pieces of unfinished wood, a saw on a table, and a dozen shelves filled with tools, screws, nails and everything he'd need to build and sculpt furniture. A set of half-finished bar stools sat stacked neatly in the corner.

"Are these all yours?" she asked, momentarily distracted by his work, amazed at how *much* of it there truly was.

"Yep," he said, moving into the space. "It's what I do when I can't sleep—which is a lot, really."

"You have trouble sleeping?" she asked him.

"Sometimes. During stressful times. Working with my hands feels more natural to me, really. More natural than real estate, if I'm honest. I like working with my hands. Like my dad. He liked working with his hands, too."

He leaned against the wall of his workshop, focused on her.

She could feel his gaze on her, watching her every move. She loved it, him studying her. She felt powerful beneath his gaze, sexy. She moved slowly, deliberately, aware of the gentle sway of her short sundress, the way it tickled the back of her thigh.

Chloe let her fingers trail down a finished but unvarnished table. "This is beautiful. I can't believe you made this." She looked at an ornate dining room chair, which had just been varnished a deep stain, one of four that would eventually go around the table. She admired the workmanship on the arms of the chair, which curved inward. He had a modern yet classic sensibility when it came to woodworking. She admired his taste.

"Why don't you try it out? You can sit on it. It's dry." He nodded toward the chair, and she sat down. "It's comfortable," she said, feeling the warm curves of the wood that seemed to be made to fit her body. She put her hands around the smooth edges of the arms of the chair. "And sturdy. You do nice work."

"Do I?" he asked, his voice sinking a little bit

lower as he crossed the room. "You look so damn sexy sitting in my chair. It makes me think I need to do some more work."

"You promised me we'd talk." She wasn't going to let him get her naked again. Not without at least a serious conversation.

"Yes, I did." He uncrossed his arms, his gaze never leaving her. She stood, uncertain. "I thought about what you said, about wanting more."

She sucked in a breath.

"And?"

He crossed the room to her. "And…I want that, too."

"You do?" Could this be true? She glanced up, confused, as he knelt down in front of her, his stark blue eyes never leaving hers. She could stare at them forever, she thought. Just like this. Then the man was on his knees in front of her, a slow grin spreading across his face. "Yes, I do. You intrigue me, Chloe Park. I want to see more of you, much more. I want more than friends and benefits."

Slowly, he put his hands on her bare knees, and she could feel the weight and heat in his palms. Then, ever so slowly, he spread her knees apart. She sucked in a breath, amazed at how quickly they'd gone from conversation to this…yet, on the other hand, part of her had expected this. Had hoped for it. The electric current that flowed between them seemed ever present, always ready to ignite from the smallest spark.

He gazed at her, focused, as his hands moved up

her skirt. He found the edges of her lacy underwear and slipped it down. She lifted her butt to help him get it off, feeling a delicious rush of the cool wood of the seat against her bare bottom. She felt frozen now, staring at this gorgeous man, sitting in the chair he made. He dipped his head and kissed her inner knee, his eyes never leaving hers as he moved slowly, ever slowly upward to her center, waxed nearly bare.

"I want you to know how special I think you are."

God, this was what she wanted. To be chosen, and yet… She wondered, what did he mean she was special? Did this mean she would be dating him exclusively?

"Of all the women I know, you're my favorite."

She felt thrilled at beating out the competition, and yet at the same time, distantly worried there still *was* competition. If she were the favorite in the harem, didn't that mean there was still a harem?

He moved upward, and she felt her body anticipate his touch, his warm, insistent lips on her delicate skin, and the questions evaporated from her mind.

He might be using sex to distract her. Might for sure be doing that. Jackson parted her inner folds with his fingers and then, gently, ever so gently, teased her with his tongue, a gentle, determined lick.

"You taste…so good," he murmured into her thigh, as his tongue sent electric bolts of desire up her spine. He lapped at her with an enthusiasm she'd never had before, and she felt her body arch to meet each swipe of his amazing tongue. Her eyes flickered closed against the rush of sensation. God, she was going to come. She was going to come...*soon*, if he kept that up.

She opened her eyes once more and found Jackson staring at her from between her legs, his eyes telling her how much he enjoyed driving her wild, how much he loved his tongue exploring her, worshipping her. Chloe couldn't look away from his face. She sucked in a breath as she watched his tongue come for her again and again, tasting her, so intimate, so...amazing. He reached up with one hand and cupped her breast through her dress, making her moan even louder.

He was so good, so very good at this. He was driving her insane with want. His words had already driven her mad, and now this...it was so good.

He hummed into her innermost depths. A hum that sent all the nerve endings in her body tingling, near exploding with pure pleasure. He picked up his pace, and she felt her pulse pound between her legs, as he nipped at skin, driving her to greater heights. She wrapped her hands in his hair just to hang on to something. Her body seemed as if it might fly off the chair, off the very ground. Suddenly, every muscle in her body stiffened, and she hit the peak of passion. Just then as he plunged his tongue into her, she came, a river of pleasure so forceful she cried out, loud, a shout of pure satisfaction, as wave after wave of an amazing climax shuddered through her, shaking her shoulders, raking her entire body.

He lifted his head, a big, accomplished grin on his face.

"Do you feel special now?" he asked her, humor dancing in his eyes.

"Uh-huh," she managed, completely spent, her legs feeling like jelly. Then he raised her up, lifting her, and moved her to his unfinished table. She went without protest, watching, amazed, as he unzipped his pants. He was ready for her, more than ready, as if making her come aroused him.

"Now it's my turn," he said, teasing her swollen folds with his oversize tip. How could she take him now, when she was so completely spent? Yet part of her wanted to, wanted to see how his massive width would feel inside her swollen, newly climaxed self. If anyone could make her come again and again, it was Jackson. *Yes*, she thought. *In me. Again. And again.* She spread her legs for him wider on the table as he teased her with his tip, his smooth knob spreading the wetness of her come across its tip. Yes. More. She wanted more. And he did, too.

Then she heard a noise. A footstep on the stair?

"Can I join in?" The strange voice startled them both and Chloe whirled in time to see a woman coming down the stairs, clad only in a trench coat she left gaping open to reveal her breasts and bare stomach.

"Laurie!" cried Jackson. "What the hell are you doing here?"

CHAPTER ELEVEN

CHLOE SCRAMBLED OFF the table, and Jackson pulled her behind him as he quickly zipped up. She glanced at the woman's blond hair and perky, bare breasts, her light pink nipples hard in the cool air-conditioning of the studio. She wore red heels, and she looked familiar, and then she remembered: this was one of the women from his phone. The one with the hourglass figure who'd sent him nude photos.

"What the hell are you doing here?" he repeated, voice low, a warning. He wasn't exactly glad to see her. Chloe was glad of that, but still confused, her heart beating madly in her chest. She felt violated. Exposed. She pressed her knees together, fiddling self-consciously with the edges of her sundress, keenly aware her G-string was on the floor near her feet.

"You always *insisted* on condoms with me, but I see *with her* it's different." Laurie frowned at Chloe, sending her a look that could cut glass. Chloe shivered, feeling the hostility radiating from the woman. Jealousy. Just-pent-up rage.

Something was off about the woman. Other than the fact that she let the trench coat come open entirely to reveal she wasn't wearing underwear, either. Her pink waxed-bare skin shone in the low light of the work studio. She was heavier in person than her pictures suggested, but more like Chloe in body type than she wanted to admit. Curvy, just like Chloe. Chloe crossed her arms in front of her, an unconscious gesture of protection.

"Laurie, you need to leave," Jackson said, a note of warning in his voice. "We're over. I told you."

Laure frowned. "Come on. I can join in. You two and...*me*. It'll be fun."

Chloe tightened her grip on Jackson's arm. No way would that be fun. No way would she...do that. Seeing him with Annaliese might have been naughty, tantalizing, but now that they'd had sex...well, she didn't want to share him. She knew that right away, the realization feeling like a frigid wind across her face. Well, at least she had boundaries. She had been wondering if, with Jackson, she'd actually had any. But here, she felt, was a full, hard stop. No threesomes. Not now. Not ever.

"How did you get in here?" Jackson kept Chloe behind him, his shoulders rigid, every one of his muscles seeming to tense.

She ignored the question. "Please. Give me a chance. I'll play—with you *and* her. I don't need you all to myself. Not at all. Just so long as I get a little taste of that magical cock of yours. Don't you want me? Don't you want both of us—at the same time?"

The idea of sharing him right now made Chloe's heart beat faster. No, she didn't want to do that. Not with this stranger. She glanced at Jackson's face, worried he wanted it.

"No, I don't." Jackson squeezed Chloe's hand in reassurance.

"I'm going to ask *one* more time. How did you get in here?"

The woman hesitated, but then came clean.

"Window. You shouldn't leave it unlocked like that." She laughed, a weird, off laugh. Suddenly, Chloe's blood ran cold. She'd *broken in*? This woman was a stalker, or deranged, or both.

"Laurie, I'm going to give you two minutes. Then I'm calling the police."

"But how can I go out like this?" She rubbed one of her own bare nipples.

Chloe glanced up at Jackson's face, seeing a look of revulsion pass across it. She was so glad to see that. This woman didn't turn him on.

"God, cover yourself," he murmured, looking away from her. Disappointed rejection crumpled her features, and she quickly wrapped the coat around her.

"Jackson…" she pleaded, all sultriness gone and in its place a crazy kind of desperation. "Please, Jackson. We need to talk. I…"

"No more talking!" Jackson snapped. "I told you, we're done."

"But I need to talk with you." She glared at Chloe. "Alone."

"No. There's nothing you have to say that I want to hear. You're going. Now." Jackson pointed to the staircase, but she didn't budge. Then he grabbed his phone from his pocket. "I'm calling the police."

Laurie's lip trembled then, and fresh tears glistened in her eyes. "No! Don't. I'm… I'm going." She cinched the belt of her coat tightly around her waist, her heels clicking on the stairs as she climbed upward.

She paused at the doorway of the studio.

"You're going to regret this," she promised, eyes on Jackson. Then she focused on Chloe, her gaze flickering up and down her curves, clearly finding her wanting. "I'd watch out if I were you. He gets bored. Easily."

"Get out." Jackson ground the words between clenched teeth.

A little ripple of fear passed over Laurie, but then she hurried out the door.

"Stay here," Jackson whispered to Chloe as he followed Laurie down the stairs. Chloe heard the door open and slam and then the *click* of the lock. Chloe's heart thudded hard in her chest as she glanced around the empty studio. She didn't know what to think, or how to feel, even as she heard Jackson moving through the first floor, hopefully to find that unlocked window and lock it. She heard him on his phone as well, giving out terse instructions to someone on the other end. All kinds of thoughts bounced around Chloe's head: Who was Laurie? Had she broken into his house before? And perhaps the most burning question of all: If Chloe *hadn't* been here, would Jackson have taken that crazy naked woman into his bed?

She wondered, was the show of kicking her out just that? Would he have acted differently had she not been there? She couldn't answer the question for herself, and doubt plagued her. She bit her lip as she remembered how he'd opened the door to Annaliese that first night, how she'd shown up wearing a jumper but nothing beneath. Surely she had to figure that half-naked and fully naked women showed up at his place all the time. Rich, gorgeous, eternally available. Why wouldn't they?

She wrestled with jealousy even as she struggled with the cold vulnerability of feeling so exposed. She shivered and hugged herself, not sure if she'd be able to get the woman's eyes out of her head, the smugness in her expression as she'd caught them. *Maybe I'm not such an exhibitionist after all*, she thought, *not if getting caught makes me feel a little bit sick to my stomach.* Or maybe the nausea was just the fact that a crazy woman had *broken in* and demanded a threesome.

"Chloe." Jackson stood at the studio door. "Are you okay?"

Chloe bit her lip, a surprising rush of emotion overtaking her: fear, jealousy, worry, embarrassment and, distantly, a sour disappointment. The woman had ruined an intimate moment, robbed her of sex with Jackson. No, she wasn't all right.

She shook her head. He crossed the room, pulling her into his arms. Reluctantly, she went, not knowing if he could provide the comfort she needed, fearing that if she really shared her feelings with him, she'd come off as too needy, too emotional. *I know other women want him. He said he wanted to date me, but did I really think the other women would go away so easily? Yet I came back for more. That makes me culpable, too.*

"I'm so very sorry," he murmured in her hair, squeezing her tight, even as she kept her arms deliberately crossed in front of her. She wasn't ready to hug him back. She felt anger and resentment, too, but she wasn't sure if she ought to be angry just at Laurie, or Jackson, or even herself. Had he been encouraging Laurie, she wondered? Had he only just made a split-second decision tonight to date her exclusively and hadn't bothered to tell anyone else? Or was it something he might just tell her and never really get rid of the other women? Did he reply to her naked picture on his phone? Praise her perky breasts so much she felt the need to come over and show them to him in person? And she also felt like kicking herself.

"Laurie is the ex I told you about," Jackson continued. "The one who tried to get pregnant without my consent."

Something hard in the pit of her stomach loosened a bit. "She was?"

"She's the last person I ever want to be with, and I've told her that, but she's not letting go." Jackson sighed. "She's sent me unwanted messages on my phone and has kept calling, and even showed up at the work party tonight. You can ask Hailey. She had to ask security to escort her from the premises."

The realization that Jackson was the victim here slowly began to sink in. "She's been stalking you?"

"Yes. I thought she might eventually stop on her own. I didn't want to get the police involved, but now…" He squeezed her tighter. "I never thought she'd do something so extreme as break in. But I'll have to get a restraining order now."

Chloe uncrossed her arms and hugged Jackson's trim waist as he squeezed her harder. He rested his chin on the top of her head.

"Why didn't you tell me she was bothering you?" Chloe asked. "I think I saw her message on your phone. I just assumed she was one of your arranged relationships, your regulars." Chloe sucked in a breath.

"You thought I wanted her?"

Chloe nodded into Jackson's chest.

"No," he said, sounding resolute. He pulled away then and stroked her cheek. "Don't you know? The only woman I truly want is you."

CHAPTER TWELVE

CHLOE COULDN'T BELIEVE her ears. Jackson was asking her to be exclusive. He'd hinted about it before, but now...now, she knew for sure: he wanted only her.

"You do?" she blurted, standing in front of him in his studio, feeling the cool wooden floor beneath her bare feet. Her head bursting with questions, her heart daring to hope it was true.

"Yes." His blue eyes shone as he traced the lines of her chin with his finger. "I just want you."

"But the women. On your phone." Not just Laurie, but the others. Annaliese, and probably many more.

Jackson looked amused. "I'll delete them, now." He took out his phone from his back pocket then and showed her his messages. There were indeed several from interested women, friends with benefits as he'd called them. One by one, he began deleting all of their contact information. He even blocked Laurie, to make a point that he truly was done with her. Chloe watched, amazed, as the women disappeared, one by one, before her eyes.

"See? I don't care about any of them, Chloe. Not since I met you. I only want to sleep with you."

"I... I don't know what to say." Chloe felt like it was all too good to be true.

"Say you'll do the same. Say you want to be with me." Jackson took both her hands. "Tell me I don't have to worry about you slipping *your* number to Kent, or anybody else."

"Kent?" Chloe echoed, and then remembered the egotistical man at the racetrack, the one who talked her ear off about himself the entire time and never asked her a single question. "Oh, no chance of that, don't worry."

"He was interested in you," Jackson pointed out.

"He can be interested all he wants. The feeling isn't mutual." Chloe was shocked to discover that Jackson, too, could be jealous. Did that mean he was really sincere? He wanted to be with her, and he wanted her to want him, too.

Jackson grinned. "I'm glad to hear that." His gaze grew serious again. "I mean it, Chloe. You're the woman I want. You're gorgeous, fun-loving, free of all inhibitions. You want to devour the world, just like I do."

She wanted to devour him, that's what she knew.

"You're the woman for me." He pulled her close then and kissed her, gently, a promise in the gesture. She kissed him back, sealing the pact. When she pulled away, she was suddenly aware of the dark corners of the studio and the fact that Laurie might be back. What if she did more than climb through an unlocked window? What if she broke in?

Chloe shivered. "Why don't we go to my place?" she offered. "Laurie doesn't know where I live. You know, just in case." She paused. "Unless you *want* another shot at Laurie and a threesome."

Jackson chuckled. "No, thanks. I don't want to share you," he said. "Not with Laurie, or anybody else."

He kissed her once more, a reassuring kiss, and she felt the knot of worry loosen in her stomach. He *picked* her. He wanted her. And she knew she wanted him just as much.

Jackson liked Chloe's apartment. It wasn't as spacious as his, but it was tastefully decorated, with clean, modern furniture. She also kept her place relatively neat, a relief for him since he liked things orderly, and clearly, so did she. They were so alike, he felt, from their sexual adventurousness to the way they approached business. He knew she worked hard from how she spoke about her job and the little he'd seen when he'd Googled her online, and she, like him, was a self-starter, someone who preferred making her own way in the world rather than accepting a traditional job with a traditional boss.

Chloe glanced at her phone and frowned.

"Do you mind if I check email really quick? I've got a client who needs an update," she said, booting up her laptop. As he watched her work, despite all that had happened that evening, he felt a surge of appreciation.

"I admire you," Jackson said as he glanced at the tidy apartment, with her laptop open on her table.

"Why?" Chloe sounded taken aback, surprised even as she paused at the keyboard.

"Well, you've made a decent living on your own." He nodded to the laptop. "I had my father's insurance money to work with, but you've built a business from scratch."

Chloe grinned, looking a little embarrassed, but also a little proud. "I guess so."

"I mean it. You're on your own, freelancing, making ends meet. You're paying your bills. You're a go-getter. I'm impressed." Of late, Jackson's dates either had no ambition, or their ambition revolved solely around getting him to propose or getting pregnant with his baby. He liked a woman who had her own life, who had goals that had nothing to do with him or his bank account.

"I love what I do, and I love setting my own hours," she said.

"Working for yourself is hard," he said. "It requires a lot of discipline." He leaned against her breakfast bar. "Like replying to an email on a Saturday night."

"Well, my clients don't sleep." She shrugged. She typed a response quickly and then sent it off. "There, I'm off the clock now."

"Good," he said as she stood. He studied her, her beautiful curves, the way her dark hair shone beneath the lights of her kitchen. So dark, so glossy. "So, I am curious about something. Why didn't you take the prize money today?"

He patted his jacket pocket, where he'd been carrying the $10,000. He realized it had been a little careless to keep that much money on him, and yet truly, the amount was pretty small for him. His own bank account had many more zeros attached.

"It wasn't mine," she said. "That money is yours."

"Every other woman I've ever dated would've taken that envelope," he said. "They wouldn't wait to be asked twice."

"It's not my money," she reiterated, sounding more resolute this time. "I earn what I keep." She nodded at her laptop. "That's what my parents taught me, and I believe it."

She swept her shining, reed-straight hair off one shoulder. He wanted to touch her, feel the softness of her skin.

"So you won't take the money, but I want to hire you, remember? As a social media consultant? Consider this a retainer." He pulled the packet out of his pocket and handed her the thick manila envelope.

She glanced at him, mouth agape. "I usually charge by the hour *after* I do the work," she said.

"Well, consider this an advance." He grinned. "Come on. Take it."

She hesitated, then eventually, tentatively, took it. "I'll make an accounting of *all* my work for you, and I'll account for every penny of this."

"I know you will." Jackson glanced at the kitchen counter, and that's when he noticed a letter from Kent Realty. He frowned and picked up the already-opened letter.

"You read this?" he asked her, holding up the envelope. "This is from Kent's company. The man you met tonight."

"It is?" She looked surprised. "So *he's* the one I'm sending rent checks to now? If I'd known, I would've asked him to knock off a hundred dollars." She laughed a little at her own joke, but Jackson wasn't in the mood for laughing.

"Mind if I look?"

"Help yourself," she said, and he skimmed the letter. Kent planned to up rents by nearly 30 percent when she renewed, which was highway robbery. No doubt he wanted the rent value on paper so that he could try to gouge Jackson in the negotiations. Underhanded tricks.

"This isn't right," he said.

"I know," Chloe said. "But, I was already thinking about moving."

The thought made Jackson snap to attention. "You can't move."

Chloe grinned. "I can't?"

"No! Not unless you move into my bed."

Chloe quirked a playful eyebrow. "Is that an official invitation?"

"A standing invitation," Jackson offered, and pulled Chloe into his arms for a kiss.

CHAPTER THIRTEEN

CHLOE WOKE IN her own bed with Jackson spooning her from behind, both of them naked, though, she remembered, they'd fallen asleep almost as soon as they'd lain down the night before—each of them exhausted from their long day and from the stress of the break-in. Somehow, wrapped up in Jackson's arms, waking with him, felt more intimate than even their hot sex at the racetrack yesterday. He stirred behind her, shifting slightly against her back.

"Morning, gorgeous," he whispered in her ear, squeezing her tightly. She turned, rolling around in his arms so she could face him. His eyes were so starkly blue.

"Morning," she echoed, snuggling up to his thick, muscular chest. The man was all hard ridges, all muscle, and she felt protected in his arms.

"I think *he* also wanted to say good morning." Jackson pushed against her, and she could feel his thick hardness resting against her belly.

"Well, good *morning*." She reached down and wrapped her hand around him, and he groaned in appreciation as she worked the length of him, her hand steady, knowledgeable, sure.

"At that rate, we're never going to get to brunch," he said.

"Brunch can wait." She ducked down beneath the sheets, determined to drive him just as wild as he'd done her the day before in his wood workshop.

She flicked her tongue across his wide tip. He rolled over on his back.

"Oh, Chloe," he murmured, and she felt a little jolt of delight. She remembered Annaliese that first night taking him in her mouth. She knew he liked that, and she wanted to please him. She wanted to be better than Annaliese, better than Laurie, better than any other woman he'd ever had. She wanted to give him everything. The rush of competitiveness surprised her, and yet she wanted to erase all other women from his mind. She wanted to make sure he didn't regret his choice.

She took his tip in her mouth, working her tongue around it, amazed at how little of him filled up her entire mouth. Chloe used both hands to work his shaft and celebrated as he grew harder with each movement.

"You're so good at that," he said, running his fingers through her thick hair, grabbing it up into a ponytail and giving it a little tug. He urged her to go faster, and she did, taking what she could. "Yes, Chloe. Oh, God, yes."

She worked to take more of him, not sure she

could, but then, in a burst of white-hot heat, he came, so deep down her throat she couldn't help but swallow. She rolled off him, panting, but he took her in his arms and kissed her.

"That's one helluva good morning," he declared, and she laughed.

They spent a lazy Sunday together, first walking to brunch at a nearby café, and then strolling through a farmers' market, with Jackson warmly holding her hand. Laurie's intrusion receded to the back of Jackson's mind. He'd instructed his lawyer to look into a restraining order, which she'd promised to do, and now he was able to just enjoy time with Chloe. The more time he spent with her, the more he was convinced that she was *the one*. She'd even taken one of her pills from her pack in front of him. He felt reassured: she was on the Pill. Unless she was going much further than Laurie ever did to trap him. His gut told him that Chloe was nothing at all like Laurie.

He felt comfortable with her, more so than he had with any other woman. She was one of the first women he'd ever met who felt like his true equal. Of course, part of him still felt guarded. He wasn't used to trusting anyone, especially not women, and the feeling didn't come naturally. The warm summer's day cooled toward the evening as a breeze rolled in from Lake Michigan, and the two moved their marathon date to his rooftop deck, where he grilled up some chicken skewers and roasted vegetables as they both sipped wine.

"This has been the perfect date," Jackson said.

"And the longest," Chloe pointed out. They'd been together for most of a weekend, and yet it had felt like no time had passed at all. Jackson wasn't the least bit edgy or tired of Chloe's company, and the more time he spent with her, the more he wanted to spend.

"True. This might be the longest date I've ever been on," Jackson admitted.

"I figured, since I think the Annaliese date was under an hour," she joked, and Jackson had to laugh. He loved her humor, her playful teasing. He deserved it, all the grief she could give him.

As he turned over the roasted veggies wrapped tightly in tinfoil on the grill, his phone pinged with an incoming message. He glanced over and saw Chloe lighting a citronella candle, as he checked his phone.

You up for a little naked time?

He frowned at the message, not sure who it came from since he deleted his contacts.

Sorry. No can do. In a relationship now.

Oh—good luck, then. If it doesn't work out, ping me.

Jackson had no intention of it not working out. He slipped the phone into his pocket. It would be quite a change, he realized, slowly weeding out the women he'd been using in his life as fillers, and yet it didn't feel like a sacrifice. He wanted Chloe to know she was the woman for him, and he didn't want women who didn't mean much to him to scare her off. For the first time in a long time, he was beginning to feel hopeful that maybe he'd found his match. Jackson had never considered himself a romantic, but as he glanced at Chloe's profile in the warm light of the summer sunset, he wondered if he'd been wrong about himself. Maybe he'd just never met the right woman.

"What is it?" asked Chloe, seeming to feel suddenly self-conscious beneath his gaze.

"You," he said. "You're so beautiful. So perfect."

"I'm not perfect. Not by a long shot." Chloe laughed uneasily. "My ex-boyfriend used to say that I was lazy, which was why I worked from home. He thought I didn't have the competitive edge or the know-how to work for a 'real' company."

"Your ex was an idiot," Jackson said, feeling anger welling up in him. "It's far harder to work for yourself. And scarier, too." Jackson studied her a second. "Was that the reason the relationship didn't work out?"

"Kevin was cheating on me," she said, simply. "He felt entitled to, I guess."

"Forget me saying he's an idiot. He's also a fool."

Chloe took a step closer to Jackson, and he folded her into a side hug, pulling her into him. He wanted to protect her suddenly from everything that could possibly hurt her. He wanted to make sure she was safe.

"He never really knew you, it sounds like," Jackson said as he took the food off the grill, onto waiting serving platters. Chloe helped him carry it to the table they'd already set, with a candle flickering in the middle. "Like my exes never really knew me."

Chloe nodded. "I think you're right." Chloe bit her lip, the slightest hint of a worry line etched into her forehead as she slid into her seat across from Jackson.

"What's wrong?"

"Speaking of exes, do you think Laurie will be back? It was so…weird. Yesterday."

"I'm sorry about that," Jackson said. "Truly. If I'd known she was that unhinged… Well, I would've acted sooner."

Chloe glanced at Jackson, the candlelight warming her features as the sky above them turned a cool purple as the sun dipped below the horizon.

"And…how do I ask this…" Chloe pushed the spaghetti strap of her sundress up one shoulder. Then she took a big breath. "Had you…I mean, been leading her on at all?"

His sharp blue eyes met hers.

"No, I hadn't."

"She wasn't a…friend with benefits?" Jackson could see how much Chloe had been thinking about this. It concerned her, and all he wanted to do was reassure her.

"No, absolutely not. The last time I saw her in any kind of romantic way was three months ago, when I caught her in the bathroom, pouring our used condom into her...well, you know."

Chloe looked relieved. "Good," she said.

Jackson reached out and grabbed her hand. "I've told everyone else on my phone that I'm in a relationship now. If you want to look at my phone, here." He offered it up to her. "I mean it, I have nothing to hide."

"I believe you," she said, and squeezed his hand. He squeezed hers back as they dug into the warm meal in front of them. Jackson was already thinking about the next day, a busy workday in another busy workweek, wondering how he'd manage to squeeze Chloe into his schedule, but already determined to find a way. Dinner flew by, and the sky darkened around them. Above them, stars shone in the cloudless sky. He poured them more wine, and then they moved over to the cushioned outdoor love seat in the far corner of his roof. The air held a slight chill as the moon rose in the sky. Jackson lit the small fire pit, and the warming smell of a small campfire filled the night air. Despite the fact that they sat on a city rooftop, surrounded by other buildings, it felt solitary, as if they were the only two people in the world.

"Now all we need are s'mores," Chloe said, snuggling into the crook of Jackson's arm as they both stared at the small orange flames.

"I think all I have are protein bars," he said, and they both laughed.

"Somehow, I don't think that would be the same."

Jackson agreed, hugging her close as the two finished their wine. Chloe looked up at Jackson and he felt, once more, awed by her beauty. He took her now-empty wineglass from her hand and put it on the table with his.

"Do you think we're moving too fast?" Chloe asked him, a note of anxiousness in her voice. He realized they had moved quickly, but he also thought of himself as a man who knew what he wanted. And right now, that was Chloe.

"When you know, you know," Jackson said, tracing her delicate chin with his finger.

He dipped down to kiss her lips, and she met him halfway. Her lips, warm and willing, parted for him, and he tasted her once more, the hint of the blackberry in the residue of wine on her tongue. The instant their lips met, he felt the rise of his desire for her, as he deepened the kiss. His want for her knew no bounds, and he wondered distantly if a fire that burned this hot would burn itself out…or if it would continue to blaze. Still, all he knew was that he wanted her again, right here, beneath the stars.

The fire pit began to die down, and the shadows grew larger on the patio, and it felt oddly safe there.

He glanced at her and grinned. "What do you say to a little exhibitionism?"

She laughed a little. "I'd say…hell, yes."

He moved closer to her. He ran his hand up the edge of her skirt as she straddled him. One of her straps fell down one shoulder, and he kissed her bare skin where it had once been. He inhaled her scent, with a hint of honey vanilla, and put his hands on her hips as she pushed her warm center against him, the heat there unmistakable. Just the small business of his gym shorts and her underwear worked as a barrier between them.

She broke free of the kiss, gasping. "We're going to get arrested if we keep this up. For public indecency."

"Not if we're quick," he murmured back, determined not to wait a second longer for her.

Her lips found his again as her nails raked his scalp, and his whole body came alive. He felt her soft breasts against him and couldn't help himself. He tugged down the front of her elastic sundress and found her braless, his mouth claiming her nipple. She moaned, arching her back, and he sucked her as her whole body became taut with need. Yes, he thought. This woman, every day. Every night. She was so responsive, so full of fire. It would take years and maybe even decades before he'd tire of this magnificent body. The stars above them twinkled as her bare breasts were now both exposed to the night. She didn't seem to care, and that thrilled him. He wanted her and wanted the whole city to know.

Let someone call the police. He'd be long finished before they arrived.

He moved her slightly so that he could nudge the elastic waistband of his shorts down, revealing that he was more than ready. Beneath the cover of her skirt, he gently rubbed against her, against the thin barrier of her thong. He almost felt like he might come just like that.

He hesitated a moment, remembering how perfect she'd felt when he'd been bare, remembering his sour disappointment when he'd come on her belly. Would he come inside her this time? Would he feel her around him when he came? The idea almost made him climax right then, and he wasn't even inside her yet. *This woman*, he thought, *this woman drives me mad.* Chloe straddled him once more, moving her thong aside with one finger, letting him past the last remaining barrier. So easy. So right. Their passion was shielded by her skirt, her bare nipples puckering in the moonlight. In the dying light of the fire pit, he saw desire in her eyes as she took him deeper inside her slick, warm center. She was ready for him, oh so ready. Chloe rode him slowly at first, teasing him, every little movement like agony. He wanted hard and fast, but she was going to put that off for as long as possible. A small smile spread across her pink lips, and in that moment, deep inside her, Jackson had never loved a woman more.

CHAPTER FOURTEEN

THE NIGHT BELONGED to them, Chloe thought, as she sat astride Jackson, not caring about who might see them. She'd never felt as primal, as animalistic, as she did now, with Jackson, beneath the stars. Growing impatient with the pace, Jackson lifted her off, flipping her around so she was on her knees, back to him on the cushy outdoor sofa. Distantly, below on the street, a cab honked at a car cutting into his lane, but neither cared about the sounds of traffic below. The drivers couldn't see them. He moved behind her and she grasped the back cushions, feeling suddenly vulnerable as he grabbed the hem of her skirt and flung it upward, the night air whisking across her bare back, her thighs exposed to the slight chill. He tugged off her thong, tired, she thought, of moving around it, and it hit his wooden deck with a tiny whisper of the elastic fabric on wood. Now she was completely bare in the night air. Her knees shook as she anticipated him, and he delivered, thrusting into her with shocking determination. She gasped as she took the whole length and width of him, completely bare, clutching the back of the couch for support. So big, she thought. So very big. Her knuckles went white.

"I've never felt like this with anybody," Jackson whispered in her ear. "Do you feel that?" He pushed harder inside her, deeper. "I'm home here. I'm meant to be here."

"Yes," she murmured. *In me. Always in me.*

"You're the woman for me," he murmured, sending her heart racing, the pulse between her legs ticking upward, even as he stretched her, filled her. She was going to come right then, come a thousand times more, too. She burned for him, even as she felt her swollen clit protest, begging for attention.

"Touch me," she asked him, voice husky and low.

He obliged, reaching around with his right hand, finding her ready for him, as he gently caressed her bundle of nerves with the pad of his finger. The sensation blinded her. Yes, this was what she needed. Him inside her. Him touching her. He picked up the pace instinctively, and she came with a violent shudder, losing every last ounce of control as the spasms took her. He didn't last much longer after that, coming with a primal grunt. She realized with a shock that he came inside her. He didn't withdraw this time, and it made her feel as if this moment were something special. He was trusting her in a way he'd told her he never trusted before.

She hoped his climax was as amazing as hers, even as she replayed his words in her mind: *I'm home here*. Yes, that's what she felt like, too. *I'm home with you*.

He slowly withdrew with a shuddering sigh, and she felt what he'd left for her, his thick, wet want between her legs, and she felt an animalistic kind of satisfaction with that, too. She realized she wanted his come; she'd always wanted his come. He said nothing about the fact that he'd come inside her, about what this meant. Instead, he pulled his shorts up, and instantly she missed the warmth of his body. She tugged her skirt down, her legs feeling the wet combination of their primal need mingling together on her inner thigh. It made her feel both naughty and fearless all at once. She pulled up her neckline, tucking herself back into the top of her dress.

Chloe gazed about the roof, noticing a few lit windows nearby with shades drawn. She hoped nobody had seen, and yet at the same time, she knew she'd do it again in a heartbeat. She liked the feeling Jackson fueled in her, a recklessness. And now she knew he trusted her. He'd told her he felt at home with her. It's more than she could've ever imagined. The cool summer wind picked up, and she shivered, acutely missing the lack of Jackson's body heat.

"Let's go inside," he offered, leading her back in his house, his hand laid protectively on the small of her back.

When she offered to head back to her apartment for the night, he wouldn't hear of it, instead insisting she stay in his bed. They slept, limbs entwined, and Chloe felt her heart fill with love.

Jackson slept the night, but woke early, loving seeing Chloe in his bed. She slept hard, her long dark hair spreading across her bare back as she lay on her stomach, naked beneath his thick cotton sheets. This was what he wanted, he realized, her in his bed every morning and every night. She belonged here, next to him. He watched her sleep, her thick dark lashes against her rosy cheeks, her thick lips slightly parted. She was so vulnerable there, so childlike. He wondered if their children would have her dark hair or his dirty-blond waves.

Their children. What was happening to him? Already he was imagining babies! Yet the thought wasn't scary in the least. Chloe just felt…right. They belonged together, and so babies, marriage, they just came with the territory. Sure, they'd only been dating a short time, but every fiber of his being told him *she* was the one. The only one.

Jackson traced her bare shoulder with one finger, amazed at the softness of her skin. She stirred then, her eyes flickering open.

"Good morning," she murmured sleepily as she rolled over, demurely covering herself with a sheet. "What time is it?"

"Seven," he said.

She yawned and stretched. "Do you need to head

to work? I've got a phone conference at nine, but I'm free till then."

"I have to be in the office at eight. But I have time to make you a quick breakfast."

"You don't have to," she said.

"I know I don't, but I want to." He grinned and kissed her on the nose.

Chloe tucked the covers around her and seemed suddenly shy. "Do you have…a, uh…shirt I can borrow?"

He tossed her a concert tee, and she pulled it over her head. She stood and it fell to her midthigh, and he'd never seen one of his shirts look sexier. He kissed her then at the foot of his bed. Their tongues met, and all he wanted to do was throw the shirt over her head and get her right back into bed.

"Wait…" she said. "Work. Breakfast. We can't…"

He glanced at the clock. No, they didn't really have time. Not for what he wanted to do to her. That would have to wait.

Ten minutes later he served up a plate full of scrambled eggs and toast, as well as a steaming cup of coffee. Chloe dug in and so did he, just glad to spend a little extra time with her before they went their separate ways. He watched her eat a mouthful of scrambled eggs.

"You're beautiful, you know that?"

"You can't be serious," she mumbled, mouth full. She pointed to her bedhead and her lack of makeup. "I can't look anywhere *near* beautiful."

"You do to me."

Chloe swallowed as he studied her. God, she was beautiful. She didn't need makeup or, hell, even combed hair. She was the most beautiful woman on earth, even as she self-consciously swiped at her mouth with a napkin.

"I love you, Chloe," he said then, the feeling welling up in him.

"You…what?" Chloe stared at him, shocked.

"I love you."

"That's what I thought you said." He could see the confusion on her face as she struggled with what to say. He knew she wasn't ready. Not yet. That was okay.

"You don't have to love me back, at least not now," he said. "But I promise you, you will." He dipped down and kissed her then, and she kissed him back.

Eventually, the lovers parted—Chloe to head back to her apartment to work, and Jackson to go into his office for a set of meetings he couldn't avoid. Jackson promised to call her later, already trying to work her into his busy schedule. When he arrived to work he was humming, in the best mood he'd been in months, maybe even years. For the first time since his business really took off, he felt the pieces of his life falling into place. He'd found a woman who might truly be a real partner, and for the first time he allowed himself to think of what that might mean: settling down, maybe having a family. The idea intrigued him. He'd always wanted to get married someday, but after all his disappointments he had worried he wouldn't ever find a woman who loved him for *him*, not his money.

He greeted Hailey outside his office, but she looked withdrawn, even a little pale.

"Morning, Hailey. Something wrong?"

"Well, sir…" Hailey looked uncharacteristically flustered. She wouldn't make eye contact with him. "Laurie is here to see you."

Jackson felt his blood boil. He glanced through the glass doors of his office and saw Laurie there, sitting in *his* desk chair, moving pens around his desk. "Why didn't you show her out? We're working on a restraining order and…"

"I think you should talk to her, sir. She said…"

"I don't care what she said. She's not welcome here or at any of my other properties. I'm disappointed in you, Hailey. I'll show her out myself." He headed to his office door, determined to give Laurie a piece of his mind, and maybe even have her arrested.

"But…sir…" Hailey seemed so very uncomfortable. There was something his assistant wasn't telling him.

"What?" Annoyance laced his voice. The last person he wanted to deal with this morning was Laurie. The fact that Hailey had failed at her job as gatekeeper irked him. Normally, she was so on top of things. He wondered what had made her hesitate.

Hailey moved closer, her voice barely above a whisper. "The woman said she's pregnant, sir. With your baby."

CHAPTER FIFTEEN

JACKSON FELT LIKE he'd been slammed in the chest with a truckload of bricks. This couldn't be true. Laurie couldn't be pregnant with his baby. He hadn't even been with her for three months, and then he'd caught her before she'd successfully poured the contents of the condom inside her…hadn't he?

"Uh. I'll take care of this. Thank you, Hailey." His assistant looked up at him with a pained expression. He wanted to tell her it wasn't true, but first he had to find out what the hell was going on. "I'll talk to her."

"I thought you would, sir. It's why I didn't see her out." Hailey's face flushed.

"You did the right thing. Thank you."

Hailey nodded, but looked sad as she returned to her desk, still not meeting his eyes. She knew as well as he did that he didn't love Laurie. That she was the last woman on earth he'd pick for a biological tie.

"Hello, Jackson," Laurie purred as he swung open the door, looking a tad bit contrite. "I tried to tell you. I said I wanted to talk to you alone. When I came to your place."

She had, he guessed, not that it mattered now. Laurie spoke in a heated rush, as if the way she delivered the news somehow was what she got wrong, and not deceiving him in the worst possible way for the worst possible reason: greed.

"Look, I know this isn't what you want, but now that I'm pregnant…well." She took a deep breath. "Let's try to work together. For the baby's sake."

She gently placed a manicured hand on her abdomen.

"Drop the act, please. I know you don't care about that baby other than what the child support will buy you."

"That is the worst thing I ever heard!" she cried. "You don't really think I'm that horrible, do you?" She blinked fast. It would've been convincing, except he knew it was a lie. Deep down, he knew. She twisted her hands together. "I love you, Jackson. That's why I want to have your baby."

"No, you don't." He shook his head fiercely. "Would you love me if I were poor?"

"Of course."

"Good," he said. "Then I'll give away all my money tomorrow. Your child support will be 20 percent of nothing."

For a split second, Laurie blanched. "See?" he said, reading her expression. "It's the money you care about."

Laurie sat down. "No, it's just that I'm feeling light-headed. With the baby."

Jackson laughed a little. Even now, she was pretending. "How did this happen?"

Laurie giggled, as she swung his swiveling chair back and forth.

"Well, you don't think I only did that trick with the condom *that one time*, did you?"

Now Jackson's blood ran cold. "You told me that was the first and only time you did that. When I caught you."

Laurie laughed and then arranged her features into a girlish pout. "Oops! I lied."

Jackson mouth was dry. Anger and panic welled up in him.

Jackson felt blindsided and betrayed—again— and yet he had only himself to blame. Why had he believed her when she told him it was just the one time with the condom? Why would he be so trusting of a woman who'd been out to trick him from the start? He knew why. Because he desperately wanted that lie to be true. He didn't want to think about what would've happened if she'd been doing that *every* time they had sex. Now, of course, he remembered her quick escapes to the bathroom regularly, the same bathroom he'd used to dispose of the condoms, before he got into the habit of flushing them. He'd chosen to turn a blind eye to those facts. And now... now... His head whirled with a dark future: a baby with a woman he didn't love and who was just after child support. And what about Chloe? How would she react if she found out Laurie was pregnant?

Jackson felt light-headed. He stumbled to a chair and sat down.

"Are you sure you're…pregnant?"

Laurie reached into her bag and pulled out a Ziploc filled with two used pregnancy tests. They both had positive pink plus signs.

"I could take another one, here, if you want me to." She pulled out a brand-new boxed test.

"N-no. Not necessary." This was a nightmare, a nightmare from which he badly wanted to wake up.

Laurie stood and came around the desk, approaching Jackson. She trailed a bright pink nail up the arm of his chair. She was wearing a too-short sundress that barely covered her backside. She was all curves. He'd been attracted to her softness, her big breasts and bigger backside, when they first met at the bar where she worked, but now being so close to her just made him feel sick to his stomach.

"I'm so happy I'll be having your baby," she said. "You've made me so happy."

Jackson couldn't think. Couldn't do anything but stare at her fake eyelashes, at everything about her that was fake, a lie. She played with the hem of her skirt, raising it a little higher. She stood with her back to the glass office door, and she pulled up the hem of her skirt high enough to show him she wasn't wearing any underwear.

"You can come in me now. Won't make any difference. We could close those blinds so that slut of an assistant won't see us, and you could do me right

here. You should at least get to bareback me, officially."

She grinned at him, and he felt like he was going
to throw up.

"Get out," he said finally, the idea of having sex
with her ever again making him feel disgusted.

"What? I thought you liked ditching condoms
now. Like with that new girl of yours. She's a little
whore, isn't she? I saw you two. I remember."

Jackson felt raw repulsion creep up the back of
his neck. She was still a stalker, still imbalanced.
Capable of anything. And now, pregnant.

She took a small step closer. "I can be your little
whore, too. If that's what you want."

With her back to the door, Laurie reached down
and slipped her own hand down between her legs,
beneath the hem of her skirt. It was obvious she was
touching herself. He felt anger surge in him and dis-
gust.

"Come on. It won't hurt the baby. Come inside
me, Jackson."

"I mean it, Laurie. You need to leave." He stood
up. She shrank back a bit. He felt a rush of emotions:
anger, resentment…even hate. This woman was ru-
ining his life. He couldn't look at her anymore. He
couldn't even be in the same room with her.

"Is this how you treat the mother of your child?"

"Just go." Jackson glared at the floor. Thankfully,
she took the cue and grabbed her purse, slinking to
the doorway.

"Jackson. I need money. Say, five hundred dollars? Just to get me by…"

"Get *out*," he ground out.

"Well…I'll let you think about all this and then maybe you'll come to your senses and do the right thing…before I have to get a lawyer involved. I'll be in touch," she promised as she walked out the door. Unfortunately, Jackson knew that was no idle threat. Thoughts of a restraining order disappeared from his mind. If she was pregnant with his child, could he still ask the courts to keep her away?

He watched her head to the elevator bank, and as soon as she disappeared behind sliding doors, he picked up his phone and dialed Hailey's extension. "Thanks…uh, Hailey, for…uh…your discretion," he said, realizing how awkward that must have been for his poor assistant to hear his ex-girlfriend announce she's pregnant. "Can you set up a meeting with my lawyer? As soon as possible, please."

Jackson's lawyer, Diane Corley, a heavyset woman in her fifties who wore her salt-and-pepper hair cut short, listened to his story and then shook her head slowly as she sat across from him in his office, the door closed behind her.

"Well, the problem is, there's no law against what she's done," she said, pushing up her tortoise-shell glasses. She took the news that a woman had tricked Jackson into a pregnancy without blinking an eye. She was tough as nails and wasn't easily rattled. "And even if there were, it would be your word against hers. She'd say you wanted her to be pregnant, or at the very least you engaged in reckless sex."

"I wore a condom every time!" he declared, balling up his fists.

"Yes, but condoms fail. There's a known risk with intercourse." Diane shook her head. "I mean, you've had sex ed. You must know this. Even if she hadn't… done what she did, the condom could've still failed. Sex is always a calculated risk."

"I know." Jackson sighed. He'd made the biggest mistake of his life ever having sex with Laurie. How he wished he could take it back. But he also knew he had taken the risks. Condoms do break. *Or they're used in ways I never condoned.*

"It just feels like a violation. There was no consent here." He stood and paced behind his desk. "Is there anything we can do? Can we have her arrested for the break-in?"

"Maybe. I'll look into it," she said.

He shook his head. He hated that Laurie had made *another* mess. He rubbed his eyes. "What *can* we do?"

Diane thought about this a moment. She tapped her pen on his desk as she sat across from him in his realty office, the door tightly shut behind him. She'd rearranged her afternoon schedule to come see him, and for that, he was grateful. "Well, first of all, we have to make sure the baby is yours."

"You think she was sleeping with someone else? She was *trying* to get pregnant by me." He paced behind his desk, feeling like a caged lion.

"Someone like that, who knows? She's clearly disturbed, so who knows what she was doing? In any case, we can use the courts to ask her to get a noninvasive paternity test, especially since she's liable to be coming after you for half the pregnancy care costs."

Jackson nodded. "Good. Well then, that's a start. But what if it's mine?"

Diane slowly shook her head. "Then she'll get 20 percent of your income, and probably all the kid's healthcare and college taken care of." She quirked an eyebrow over her glasses. "Would you want to see the kid?"

Jackson thought about this. It wasn't the baby's fault he'd been too trusting of his gold-digging mother. Yet he also despised Laurie. How could that all work? But what about Chloe? How would she feel if he had a relationship with a child who wasn't hers? The thought of even *telling* Chloe about this made him feel sick.

"I don't know." Then he thought about an innocent child, about how it wouldn't be his or her fault who his mother was, or how she'd come to be. "Yes, I think I would. I couldn't abandon the child. It's not his fault."

"Even if it means alienating your new girl. What's her name?"

"Chloe. Her name is Chloe."

"Right, Chloe. Does she know yet?"

"No." Jackson hadn't wanted to alarm her. It was bad enough they'd been interrupted by a crazy half-naked Laurie who'd broken into his house. No, Jackson didn't want her to know. Didn't want her to know as long as it was possible not to know. "Like you said, what if the baby's not mine?"

"What if it is?" Diane asked him.

CHAPTER SIXTEEN

A COUPLE OF weeks passed, and Chloe noticed that Jackson seemed distant and distracted. He still texted Chloe often, and they dined together a few times, but work seemed to keep him away from her, and she felt a distance creeping between them and wondered why. Chloe thought things might be turning around when he invited her to Untitled, a bustling restaurant downtown in the basement of a building in River North, modeled after an old Al Capone speakeasy, built in the days of Prohibition. On the outside, the door was a simple black; on the inside, there was a thriving bar and restaurant, with a giant portrait of Capone sitting near the stairs.

It felt odd almost, being hidden away in the restaurant without a storefront or sign. They were surrounded by people in the dining room, and yet the place felt secretive. Dark. On the drive over, Chloe already felt Jackson's distance from her. He seemed disengaged as he stared out the window of the limo driven by his driver. His mood hadn't changed when they'd sat down in the restaurant and ordered wine and their meal. Making conversation felt like pulling teeth, and Chloe wanted to know why everything felt so heavy. She'd asked him at least twice what was bothering him, but both times he'd told her nothing. She knew he was lying.

"Something wrong?" she asked him—for the third time—seeing he'd barely touched his steak, a meal that Chloe realized wouldn't be cheap. In addition to the steak, he'd ordered one of the most expensive bottles of red wine on the menu.

"Nothing," he said, and she got the feeling he might be lying. His phone pinged, and he grabbed it, glancing at it with interest.

"Who's that?" Chloe's inner insecurities popped up. Was that one of the women on his phone? She knew they occasionally still texted, even though he'd deleted their contact information. Should she ask him to block them? Or should she just trust that he'd say no every time?

"Just…work stuff." Jackson frowned as he glanced at the screen.

She knew he wasn't telling her the truth. It was the same gut feeling she had about Kevin when he'd made excuses about working late in the weeks leading up to their breakup. If it was one thing Chloe knew, it was that her instincts were rarely wrong. Jackson was hiding something. The question was: What?

Maybe he's not ready to be faithful, a little voice told her. *Maybe he's chafing at being in a relation-*

ship with one woman. Maybe he doesn't actually like telling all those other women no. Or hell, maybe he's not telling them no.

Chloe mentally shook herself as she reminded herself not to jump to conclusions or find Jackson guilty in the court of her own mind without any proof at all.

"Hey, you know you can talk to me," she said. "About…anything." *Share with me. Whatever it is, we can work out. Just don't shut me out.*

"I know I can." Jackson glanced up at her, as she'd temporarily diverted his attention away from his phone's screen. "Sorry. I just need to…" He tapped out a response on his phone.

Jealousy flared in her mind. Was he texting an old girlfriend? A friend with benefits? Had he gotten another naked photo—this one he couldn't resist? Her mind was one runaway train, careering down the tracks, no brakes and no engineer at the helm. She needed to get a grip on herself. He'd promised he wasn't going to see anyone else, but what if he was growing tired of her? What if he was finding his promise harder to keep than he thought? Chloe put down her fork.

"You seem distracted tonight. Off," she said.

"I know. I'm sorry. It's just… I'll finish here, one second." He tapped more on his phone.

"If you're having doubts…" Chloe began.

"Doubts? About what?" Jackson kept his eyes on his phone. *Look at me*, she wanted to shout. She took a big gulp of their expensive wine. The complex bouquet of tastes was nearly lost on her as she was so fixated on Jackson.

"If you're having doubts about us, then just tell me." Chloe exhaled. She had to mentally prepare herself for what might be coming next. She was giving him an out.

Jackson's head bounced up, surprise on his face. "Why would I have doubts about us?" Now he looked confused. He set his phone down and reached for her hand across the table. "Chloe, you're the most amazing woman I've ever met. I don't have any doubts about you."

He squeezed her hand, and she felt a flood of relief. He seemed completely sincere. He still felt the same way. Whatever was going on with his phone didn't interfere with his feelings for her.

"Has Laurie been bothering you?" she asked.

"Why do you ask that?" He seemed a little defensive. Did the mystery texts on his phone have to do with his stalker? He eyed her warily. *What was he hiding?*

"Well, for one, she broke into your house." Chloe cocked her head, and he sent her a rueful smile. "And I wanted to know if the restraining order worked."

Jackson withdrew his hand and took a sip of his wine. He seemed uncomfortable about even the mention of Laurie at all. "Let's not talk about Laurie tonight. Let's not let her ruin our dinner."

"Okay, but…I want to help." *And I can't help if*

you don't tell me what the problems are, like when you didn't tell me about Laurie stalking you in the first place. She remembered how he'd kept that detail secret until Laurie had burst in on them. Would she have ever known he had a stalker ex if that hadn't happened?

It was one thing to ask her to be exclusive, but it was another thing to treat her like a real partner, and that meant letting her in, letting her all the way in. Yet looking at Jackson's face, Chloe felt reluctant to push it. He'd told her his off mood had nothing to do with her, but was he telling her the whole truth?

Jackson's phone dinged again, and Chloe fought the urge to snatch it from his hands and toss it across the restaurant. Jackson glanced at his screen and his eyes bulged, a flush creeping into his face. Then he tossed down his napkin on the table.

"I—I need to… I'll be right back," he stammered in a rush as he left Chloe sitting at the table, fork in hand, wondering what had just happened.

Jackson's heart pounded like the rat-a-tat-tat of a tommy gun in his chest. Laurie had sent him a picture, and not just any picture—one of Chloe and Jackson on his rooftop patio. Chloe, breasts exposed, straddled him. Her skirt covered their lower halves, but it was pretty obvious to anyone what was happening.

I was deep inside her right then, and her face, eyes closed, head back, implies it, too. The picture was taken from Chloe's building, he realized. Must have been, as the angle was from above and to the right. Had she broken into Chloe's apartment two weeks ago? The thought made Jackson's heart race even faster.

He stood beneath the bar's large open staircase as he looked at the picture once more. Laurie had sent it to him with a single message:

I need money for vitamins and a doctor's appointment for the DNA test. Send me $5,000 today or I'll tell your little whore about the baby you made inside me.

Blackmail. Of course she'd resorted to that. He'd expected nothing less of Laurie. And what kind of prenatal vitamins cost five thousand dollars? He was no fool. He knew she'd use the money on herself. Of course, five thousand dollars was nothing to him. He'd bet more on a single blackjack hand in Vegas before. At the same time, he also knew if he paid her, she'd keep asking for more. And then what?

He decided to stall.

I already paid for the DNA test. We're waiting for results, remember? No need for extra money for that.

She responded almost immediately.

I think we should do more than one DNA test, so I need $$. And your baby needs vitamins.

As he stood there pondering what to do, another message came through. There was another photo, this one showing all of Chloe's bare backside as Jackson readied to enter her.

Better decide quick, or I'll make this photo public. Maybe everybody should see how she takes you. Like the whore she is.

White-hot rage pulsed in Jackson's temples. All he wanted to do was protect Chloe from this…crazy woman. But the more he tried, the deeper the nightmare.

Don't do this, he texted back instantly.

His phone dinged again, and this time, there was a close-up shot of Chloe—all of her down below. Laurie was unstable, crazy. This nightmare needed to stop.

"What is that?" Chloe's voice behind him made him whirl. With the hum of patrons in the bar, he hadn't heard her approach, and now she was staring at his phone. Had she seen?

"Nothing," he said.

"That's a lie." Chloe's mouth twitched. "I saw it. Someone sent you a naked picture." The hurt in her eyes was real, and in that instant, Jackson realized the horrible conclusions Chloe was jumping to right then.

"It's not what you think." Jackson desperately wanted her to believe him, but not ask any more questions. What was worse? Having her believe he wanted to have sex with other women, or having her know that he might have impregnated one of them?

"Then you'd better explain." Chloe folded her arms across her chest. Her dark eyes flashed fire, but he was amazed at her calmness, her clarity. She wasn't going ballistic, or shouting and screaming, like another woman might. She was calmly waiting for an explanation even as fury burned just beneath the surface. Jackson realized he had one shot and one shot only at getting through to her before she made up her own mind. He felt like choking right then. What did he say? Anything he could think to say, even the truth, seemed like the wrong answer.

When he hesitated, Chloe tried once more. "Now is the time for you to come clean, because there won't be another chance." Jackson glanced at her, as she stood, clutch in hand, ready to flee. "Just tell me the truth, okay? Whatever it is. The truth is better than a lie."

"You might not be so sure about that when you hear it."

"Just be honest with me." Chloe swallowed hard as she took a step closer to him. Her dark eyes shone with unshed tears and the hint of pain. "If you don't want to be with me exclusively, you can tell me."

"No! That's not it. Not it at all." Jackson ran a frustrated hand through his hair. The thrum of the noise from the bar felt like nails on a chalkboard. He grabbed her elbow and moved her to the hallway to the bathroom, where the noise was a bit more muffled.

She looked at him expectantly. Pain still in her eyes.

"It's not you. It's Laurie." He took a deep breath. God, how was he going to tell her this? "The picture you saw. She took it. Of us." He showed her the picture on his phone. Starting with the close-up one and then flipping to the two of them together on his rooftop deck.

"What?" Chloe cried in shock as she studied the images. "But...how?"

"I don't know. I think she was in your building."

Chloe tried to take Jackson's phone, but he held it tightly. She pressed her face close to the photo. "I think you're right. Has to be. From that angle." Chloe glanced up at Jackson, fear on her face. "Did she break into my building?"

"I don't know. But...there's more." Jackson swallowed. "She's threatening to make the photos public."

Chloe's hands fell to her sides. "What?" Her voice sounded hollow and empty, and the color drained from her face. "But if she did that...I could lose clients. And—God! My parents might see!"

"I'm going to do everything I can to make sure the pictures don't get out."

Chloe hugged herself. "Can we have her arrested? For blackmail? Or...what's it called...revenge porn? Isn't that against the law?"

"I'll ask my lawyer about it." *You've got to tell her the rest.*

"I can't believe this. I can't believe..." Chloe shook her head. "This is a nightmare."

A nightmare that's about to get worse.

"There's something else." Chloe looked up at him, and he could see her steel herself for another blow. How he wanted to protect her from this. He wondered, briefly, if after she knew she'd even speak to him again. It was a lot to ask anybody to take. "Remember when I told you that Laurie tried to get pregnant behind my back?"

Chloe nodded, a single stiff nod. How he wished he didn't have to tell her this.

"Well, that wasn't the only time she tried. Apparently." Suddenly, Jackson couldn't look Chloe in the eye. God, how he wanted not to tell her this. "She says she's pregnant. She says she's pregnant with my baby."

CHAPTER SEVENTEEN

THE WHOLE WORLD seemed to shrink then, as Chloe watched Jackson's lips move but didn't hear anything else coming out. Laurie, crazy Laurie, was pregnant with Jackson's baby? No. God, no. Suddenly Chloe couldn't breathe. She felt like the walls of the small hallway were going to close in on her. A woman bustled out of a nearby bathroom then, brushing past them, and Chloe felt like she'd fall.

"Chloe. Say something." Jackson gripped her by her elbows, blue eyes on her, pleading for something. His thick blond hair was a little long, a little ruffled.

She felt numb. Worse than numb, empty. She wasn't even angry, although she assumed that would come later. Now she didn't feel anything.

"The baby might not be mine."

"But it might be," Chloe choked out.

"Yes." Jackson glanced at the floor. He didn't have to say more. Laurie was trying for this, on purpose, so what were the odds she was sleeping around? Panic, white-hot panic, began to rise in her throat. She'd asked Jackson to be honest with her, yet now that he had, she wasn't sure she could handle it. All the ramifications flooded her: a baby in their lives, a reminder of her, a mentally unstable stalker, who now had the important title of *mother of his child.* She remembered the crazy look in Laurie's eyes when she'd broken into his house, the twisted way she'd invited herself into their bed. She'd gotten off on it, too, somehow.

Just like you did? Watching Jackson and Annaliese? Now she felt sick to her stomach. Did she have anything in common with that crazy, horrible woman? Surely not. Yet the tiny voice wouldn't be silenced, either. *I was different,* her mind wanted to shout. *Jackson loves me. Doesn't he? He said he did. He wanted me. Not her.*

But with the baby, did that change anything? What if he decided to marry her? The thought made her feel like she couldn't breathe.

"What are you going to do?" she asked, cursing herself for lacking the courage to ask the question on her mind. Would he marry her?

"I don't know. Wait for the results of the DNA test next Tuesday," he said.

"And then? If it's yours?" Bile pooled in her throat.

"I don't know, Chloe. I really don't."

Chloe stepped away from him, and his hands fell away from her elbows.

"I… I need some time. To process all this." She glanced away from his handsome face, the hurt obvious in his eyes.

He covered his goatee with one hand, agitated, upset.

"Please. Chloe. Don't leave me." The pleading tone made tears spring to her eyes. He needed her, and yet she couldn't help him. Not like this. But what could she do? She couldn't breathe. Couldn't think. She needed to regroup. To figure out what she would do next. How she felt about all this. She'd been the one imagining having a baby with Jackson. Not helping to raise a baby that wasn't hers. That was *if* he didn't marry Laurie.

"I just… I can't right now. I need to think." Tears choked her voice. She needed space from him. Jackson let her go.

"I guess I understand." But his eyes told a different story. They looked betrayed, abandoned. "Let me and my driver drop you home."

"No!" Chloe shook her head. "No. I want to go. Alone."

Chloe left Jackson then, running up the staircase and into the warm summer's night. She felt a surge of guilt for leaving Jackson when he needed her most, and yet she just couldn't stay. Not when her heart was breaking. Not when she didn't know if she could accept this. Tears streaked down her face as she hugged herself, jogging past a couple on the street holding hands and laughing.

Chloe stood in her empty apartment, staring out her window at Jackson's darkened living room. He hadn't come home yet, or if he had, he hadn't turned on any lights. She sat in her dark apartment, too, still feeling stunned. She just couldn't handle it. She still wasn't sure what she was going to do. Never in a million years had she imagined being faced with a choice like this.

What if he lied about her tricking him? What if he'd gone inside her, like he's been inside me?

No, she reasoned. Laurie had even *mentioned* the fact that he insisted on condoms when she'd broken into his house. Also, she'd broken into his *house*. An unstable person like that would be the kind of person who thought trapping a man with a baby was a good idea.

What if he marries her? What if he feels it's the right thing to do?

The traitorous thoughts came fast and furious, like Hydra heads. As soon as she swatted down one, two more took its place.

Even now, as she struggled with how to feel about Laurie's pregnancy, she found herself missing Jackson. Even now, her body ached for him, for his touch, for his solid arms around her shoulders. But what if she never felt them again?

Talk to him, her mind screamed. But she wasn't ready. She just couldn't face it if he told her he planned to do the right thing, if that even applied in this situation. Was the right thing marrying Laurie?

She watched as the light flickered on in Jackson's second floor, his workshop. There was just a single small window there, but through it she caught a glimpse of his shadow, and then part of his back as he sat nearby and worked on finishing one of his bar stools.

How can he work at a time like this? she wondered, but then realized he probably was trying to calm down, maybe refocus his mind. He'd told her that woodworking was soothing. He was good at it, too, working with his hands. Chloe tried not to think about what else his hands were good at doing. She got up and moved away from the window. She was going to drive herself crazy. Maybe she ought to just go over there. Talk to him.

But I still don't know how I feel about this. Any of it.

She wanted to be okay with it, but deep down, she wasn't sure she could be. She'd never imagined being a stepmom, and especially not to a child conceived like this, not in love, but greed. And then having Laurie in their lives, potentially forever. It made her sick. The whole situation made her sick to her stomach. Could she get over it? Could she somehow learn to live with it?

Maybe she could. She wanted to, for Jackson's sake. *He told me he loves me. And I think I love him, too. But was that enough?*

She wasn't sure. She truly wasn't. And if there *was* a baby involved, then she felt on some level she had to be sure. She owed it to the baby, who'd done nothing wrong here. Chloe wasn't going to commit unless she was sure she could go the distance.

She glanced at Jackson's lit window across the alley. She needed some time to think.

Tuesday morning, Jackson sat at his desk in his office overlooking Lake Michigan barely taking note of anything around him. The whole world seemed to be drained of color now that Chloe had left him. He wanted to believe she just needed time to adjust to the news, but when he didn't hear from her Saturday or Sunday or Monday, he began to worry the split wasn't temporary.

How can I blame her, really? How would I handle the news if she told me she were carrying another man's baby?

He didn't know, couldn't know, but he felt jealousy burn in his gut at the very thought. She'd no doubt feel the same.

"Knock, knock." Hailey stood at his office door, a look of pity on her face. She'd been extra nice to him recently—offering to get his dry-cleaning and other tasks he normally handled himself. He appreciated her effort. "Want another coffee? I was going to run to Starbucks."

"No, Hailey. But thank you."

Hailey hesitated. "How are you…holding up, sir?"

"Terribly," he admitted, and she smiled. "Chloe didn't take the news well."

Hailey's features softened. "Give her some time," she said. "I don't know Chloe well, but what I do know of her, I really like. She might come around."

"Thanks, Hailey." His assistant nodded once and then retreated from the doorway. Thankfully, Hailey had kept the news of the pregnancy to herself. Nobody yet was gossiping about it at work, and for that he was grateful he had such a loyal assistant. He made a mental note to up her bonus this year for a job well done.

Hailey made her way to the elevator for the coffee break and disappeared behind the sliding steel doors. Jackson tried to focus on his email, but he found his mind wandering. He couldn't focus on anything. He wondered what Chloe was doing. *How* she was doing. He picked up his cell phone and texted her. Just a quick message. How are you?

Her replies over the last two days had been curt and to the point, which he expected again. But before he could mull over that much more, he heard a knock at his door.

Kent stood there, looking predatory as usual, his blazer-and-khaki prep look solidified for yet another day. Jackson wondered if the man owned any other clothes. He frowned, not at all happy to see him.

"Ever hear of making an appointment?" Jackson felt his fingers clutch his phone as annoyance thrummed in his veins.

"You haven't been returning my calls," Kent said, grinning. "I *was* asking for a meeting, so I figured I'd take the bull by the horns." He made himself at home by sitting in one of the chairs in front of Jackson's desk and crossing his legs at the knee. "You not interested in 1209 anymore?"

Jackson sighed. Chloe's building. "Yes, I'm interested. I'm just…busy with other things at the moment."

The triumphant look on Kent's face made Jackson want to punch him square in the nose. "So I've heard."

"What do you mean, you've heard?" Now Jackson's guard was fully up.

"People talk." He put his fingers together and made a steeple. It was as if he was trying to imitate a James Bond villain. "Let's just say I heard you… weren't careful."

"What do you know?" *And who told you? Not Hailey. Not Chloe. Then who? Laurie.*

"Enough." Kent grinned. "I actually understand it. Laurie's a piece of ass. Tapped that myself."

"Wait…what?" Jackson's head spun.

"You didn't think you were the only rich guy she was trying to reel in? But I'm too smart for that, friend. I got snipped so women couldn't trap me. Then the joke's on them. You know…when they are trying for it, but all they're getting are blanks." Kent seemed proud of his little scheme, obnoxiously proud. The look on his face made Jackson disgusted. "You've got to think ahead, man. And the best part is, they beg you *not* to wear a condom."

"You're a lowlife, you know that? And why would you get that kind of serious surgery just…"

"Because I like to win, and this way, *I win*." God,

even sex was some kind of sick competition with him. "I'm just playing the players." He shrugged. "They're trying to use me, but I use them instead. It works out nicely."

Jackson felt sick to his stomach. "When did you sleep with Laurie?"

"Right before you. She'd been trying to snag a whale forever. You just happened to be the whale of the month."

"So you took advantage of her."

"Something like that." Kent crossed his legs and studied his nails absently. "Actually, you should thank me. She was so brokenhearted when I told her I'd been snipped. I told her all about you, how much you were worth and everything. She couldn't wait to meet you then. She even got a job at your favorite bar for the privilege."

Jackson felt stunned. The whole thing was a… setup? He felt like he'd been hit with a sledgehammer.

Kent was still gloating. "But I get it, it's rotten timing for you. Just when things were heating up with that sexy little number of yours. What was her name? Chloe?"

"Keep Chloe out of this." Jackson's voice was a low growl.

"Those pictures of you two on the roof…"

"Wait. You saw the pictures? That Laurie sent?"

"Saw them?" Kent laughed a little, high-pitched, and clapped his hands in glee. "I *took* them. I own that building next door. I just forwarded them on to Laurie. I knew she'd be interested. And she was."

Jackson stood up and clutched the edge of his desk. "Give me one reason why I don't throw you out of here right now."

"Because I still have the building you want. You need me."

Jackson fumed, staring at his longtime adversary. "What I want to know is why? Why even tell me all this?"

"That's easy: to gloat, New Money. Like I said, I like to *win*, and I can't win if you don't even know we were playing a game. That you lost."

"Get out," Jackson ground out, barely restraining his temper.

"You're making a mistake, New Money."

"Get the *hell* out." Jackson banged his desk with his fist and Kent stood.

"I'll chalk this up to *paternal* stress, amigo." Kent left the office, whistling. Jackson wanted to run after him and tackle the son of a bitch. Jackson shook his head. He should be glad that Laurie hadn't been crazy enough to break into Chloe's building. Kent owned it and had the common door key, so it wouldn't be hard for him to get on the roof and snap a few shots. Once again, Jackson was baffled by Kent's seeming obsession with him. Telling Laurie to go seek him out? Stalking his rooftop patio? Jackson shook his head. Seemed that Kent had nothing better to do than follow him around. Pathetic.

His temper cooled, and he found himself regaining a bit of his composure. Then his phone rang. He glanced at it and saw Chloe's name flash across the screen.

"Hey," she said, voice sounding soft, contrite even. "Do you have time for a break? I know it's not quite lunchtime, but…"

"Yes, I'll make time," he said, hope welling in his chest for the first time that morning. "Where do you want to meet?"

CHAPTER EIGHTEEN

THEY MET AT Navy Pier, where tourists thronged the pathway and the oversize Ferris wheel anchored the land side. Restaurants and little shops lined the pier, as did vendors offering boat rides to the lake. Every Saturday in the summer, the pier offered up fireworks and boat rides, but today all Jackson wanted was to see Chloe. She was sitting on a bench when he arrived. She stood, happy to see him. When Jackson opened his arms, she rushed into them, giving him a big hug. His heart swelled then. He'd missed her in the short time they'd been apart, and the worry that she was leaving him, forever, was almost too much to bear. God, she smelled so good. Her hair like lavender and vanilla. He suddenly wished they were alone.

"I'm sorry," she said into his chest.

"Why?" he asked her, perplexed as he pulled away, the two of them surrounded by people and yet very much alone at the same time.

"For…freaking out on you."

"You have every reason to freak out," he said.

"Want to sit?" She offered a place next to her on

the bench, facing out to Lake Michigan. He took a seat there, the shadow of the Ferris wheel behind them. He took her hand, still worried she might be here to deliver bad news. *I never want to see you again* bad news.

"How have you been?" he asked, feeling as stiff as his words sounded.

"Bad," she admitted. "But I've thought things through."

He took a deep breath. "And?"

"And I just wanted you to know that…" Chloe swallowed. "Whatever happens, I'm with you."

For the first time since Laurie came to his office with the horrible news, Jackson felt a tiny sprig of hope bloom in his chest.

"You're with me," he echoed. "Even if the baby is mine?"

Chloe nodded. He stared at her dark eyes, full of emotion, and felt tears welling in his own. "You're sure?" he asked, squeezing her hand.

"I'm positive. Whatever happens, we'll face it together."

Jackson pulled Chloe into his arms and kissed her deeply. "I love you," he murmured.

"I love you, too." Those words made his heart feel like it would explode. He hugged her even harder, not wanting to let her go.

"I'm sorry I took so long," she mumbled into his chest. "I just wanted to be sure."

He released her. "No, I'm glad you took some

time to think it over. I know it's not an easy decision. Not at all." He glanced back at the huge white
wheel turning slowly behind them. "Why don't we
take a ride? We deserve a break, a little fun, I think."

"You want to?" she asked, uncertain.

"I do."

The line was short, and in minutes, they'd gotten their own car, sealed from the elements by glass
windows on all sides. Jackson and Chloe sat across
from each other, gazing into each other's eyes. There
was a bit of sadness about her, but at the same time,
Chloe was the kind of woman who'd be the partner he needed: fearless. Most women would've run
away and kept running after they'd heard the news
of the pregnancy. Not Chloe. Jackson knew beyond
a doubt this woman was the one. If he had a ring in
his pocket, he would get down on one knee right
there in the Ferris wheel car and propose. As the car
moved higher and higher into the sky, giving them
a breathtaking view of the city skyline and the glistening blue lake, Jackson allowed himself to actually feel hopeful about the future.

"You've changed my life for the better, you know
that?" he told Chloe. "Standing by me, it's brave.
And I'll never forget that. I've never trusted anyone
like I trust you, and I hope you know that you're my
partner. Now and always."

"I trust you, too," Chloe said. "Thank you for
telling me about Laurie. About what was going on.
You could've kept it all from me, and…I mean, I

was mad at first that you didn't tell me right away, but I also get you were hoping the DNA test proves it's not yours." Chloe glanced at Jackson. "Do you think it's possible it's not yours?"

"Well, Kent had been sleeping with her before me, and he's had a vasectomy. Told me all about it." Jackson rolled his eyes.

"He—what?" Chloe frowned.

"Oh, yeah, and actually Kent is the one who told Laurie she ought to date me. So, small world."

Chloe's mouth dropped open. "You can't be serious."

"Unfortunately, I am. Kent hates me, always has, and has had this chip on his shoulder ever since I outmaneuvered him on a parkland deal. He's been after me ever since, and looks like he finally got me." Jackson glanced at the tiny white sailboats dotting the water of the massive lake far below them.

"No," Chloe said, grabbing Jackson's hand. "He hasn't won. Because you have me, and we'll get through this together. One way or another. I know we will."

Jackson squeezed Chloe's hand, feeling his heart swell up with love and admiration for her. She was a good woman, through and through. "Come over here," he said, grinning. He patted the seat next to him.

"Can I?" She glanced around, clearly worrying about the balance of the car.

"Then I'm coming over there." He made a quick

move and then was beside her, pulling her into his arms. The car swung a bit, but righted itself soon enough. He kissed her long and hard, their tongues meeting in a promise of more kisses to come.

He felt her hand wander down to the front of his pants.

"Looks like you might need to open that zipper," she purred in his ear, and he felt a shiver run down his spine. She was like a drug, a powerful aphrodisiac, one he was powerless to resist. He wanted her.

"Naughty girl! We're in a bubble. The *whole* city can see us."

"You were the one who turned me on to exhibitionism," she pointed out. He had to laugh.

"True. But then we were photographed and blackmailed." He quirked an eyebrow. "See how well that turned out?"

"That does put a damper on the mood," Chloe agreed.

"Then again," Jackson said, squeezing her bare knee, "maybe I should take you right here. Right now." Somehow, he knew he'd find her wet and ready.

The phone in his back pocket rang. Reluctantly, he glanced at it and saw Diane was calling.

"It's my lawyer," he told Chloe. She nodded. "Hello?" he said, and put the call on speakerphone. "Diane? I've got you on speaker. Chloe is here with me, and anything you say to me, you can say to her."

"Good. Because I've got news. The DNA test results came back."

"And?" Jackson braced himself for bad news. He felt like he'd been zapped into a Maury Povich episode. Chloe squeezed his hand.

"And you're *not* the father."

Jackson stared at Chloe, feeling a mix of emotions: relief, joy, shock. Chloe clutched at his arm.

"He's not?" Chloe could barely contain her glee. "For certain?"

"Nope. One hundred percent not Jackson's. Actually, we ran two DNA tests, since she admitted to sleeping with another person around the same time, and *that* test came up positive, so you're off the hook."

"Wait...was that other person Kent Roberts?" Jackson asked. Chloe's mouth dropped open in shock.

"I'm not technically supposed to know his name," Diane replied, "but I happened to look at the file, and the other DNA sample was labeled Roberts, so it's fairly likely."

"Well, I'll be damned." Jackson barked a bitter laugh. "Looks like he has a malpractice suit on his hands."

"A...what?" Diane asked, sounding confused.

"He had a vasectomy, but clearly it didn't take. He thought the surgery would mean he could sleep with whoever he wanted without protection. He didn't care about disease, apparently, or anything else."

"Oh, I had a case once like that," Diane said. "It's rare, but it happens. One in one thousand men regrow the tube or whatever, and then…well, the highway is open for business again, I guess." She coughed uncomfortably on the line, but Jackson didn't care. He laughed, a full-bodied laugh. Nobody deserved that nightmare more than Kent. Looked like the player got played, by his own body. Instant karma.

He felt a bubble of excitement and relief grow in his chest. He wasn't the father. He still couldn't believe it.

Jackson shook his head. "So this means I don't owe Laurie anything?"

"That's right. And if she tries to release any photos of you, we'll hit her with everything we've got. I've already served her a cease-and-desist on the photos she has, and if she releases them, we'll take her for every penny she has. So you *and* Chloe should rest easy. Plus, I've got Chicago PD looking into filing burglary and trespassing charges as well."

"Good," Chloe said.

"Thank you, Diane. Really," Jackson said.

"Anytime." Diane clicked off the line, and Jackson hugged Chloe.

"God, can you believe that?" Jackson said, shaking his head. "It's Kent's!"

"Well, looks like she's got her rich daddy after all," Chloe said, laughing a little. Her face shone with happiness and relief, and she looked so beautiful. "I can't believe he did that just so he could…you know…go without a condom. What if he decided one day he wanted kids?"

Jackson shrugged. "I guess he doesn't have to worry about that now."

The two of them laughed a little.

"They kind of deserve each other," she said.

"Hell, yes, they do," Jackson said slapping the cushioned armrest.

Chloe laced her fingers between his. "I'm not going to lie, this makes me very, very happy. Does that make me a bad person?"

"Not at all," he said. "I love you. So much." Jackson drew Chloe into his arms for a kiss. "You're the only woman I want, now and forever."

"You're sure?"

"Beyond positive." Jackson lifted Chloe up so she was sitting in his lap. He kissed her gently, and she returned the kiss. The Ferris wheel spun back by the platform slowly and then began its ascent once more to the top of the wheel. He broke the kiss and stared into her dark eyes.

"Now, where were we before we were interrupted?"

"About to break about a dozen public indecency statutes?" Chloe ran her long nails through his thick hair. He closed his eyes, loving her touch, eager to have it for many months and years to come.

"Oh, yes, that's right." Jackson slipped his hand up the side of her skirt, feeling her soft skin, thrilled with the knowledge that one day, maybe she'd be the one to carry his baby.

"I love you," she murmured, even as he worked

his hand up higher, rubbing her outer thigh and squeezing.

"I love you," he said, nuzzling her neck as she turned, straddling him in his seat. He could feel her warmth, her readiness, even through the fabric of his pants. This was exactly where he was meant to be.

Yes, he thought, *I'm coming home.*

* * * * *

COMING SOON!

We really hope you enjoyed reading this book. If you're looking for more romance, be sure to head to the shops when new books are available on

Thursday
1ˢᵗ November

LET'S TALK
Romance

For exclusive extracts, competitions
and special offers, find us online:

f facebook.com/millsandboon

⊙ @millsandboonuk

🐦 @millsandboon

Or get in touch on 0844 844 1351*

For all the latest titles coming soon, visit
millsandboon.co.uk/nextmonth